"Isn't there anyone who's on my side...?"

Sisbell Lou Nebulis IX
Third-born princess of the Nebulis Sovereignty. Possessor of Illumination, which re-creates videos of past incidents. Mostly stays locked in her room.

"I was hoping this would be a good opportunity to talk to my sister, but prospects are looking bleak…"

Aliceliese Lou Nebulis IX
Second-born princess of the Nebulis Sovereignty. Follows Sisbell here to investigate her strange behavior…

Our Last Crusade or the Rise of a New World

"Do you like my swimsuit? Isn't it cute?"

Mismis Klass
Captain of Unit 907 of the Special Defense Third Division in the Empire. Became a witch after falling into a vortex and obtaining astral power.

Independent State of Alsamira
A small country in a desert oasis located on the eastern side of the continent. Popular among tourists for its clear beaches. Neither neutral nor part of the Empire or the Sovereignty.

"Your light... What are you hiding inside you...?"

Flames rolled into the air, breaking like waves and spawning thousands of embers. Sisbell shivered when she gazed up at the wall of fire.

Iska
Member of Unit 907 of the Special Defense Third Division. A young swordsman who used to be a Saint Disciple. Reunites in Alsamira with the witch who got him dismissed from his position.

Our Last CRUSADE OR THE RISE OF A New World

4

KEI SAZANE

Illustration by
Ao Nekonabe

YEN ON
NEW YORK

Our Last CRUSADE OR THE RISE OF A New World

4 KEI SAZANE

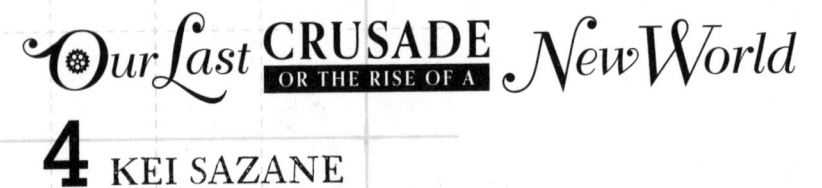

Translation by Jan Cash
Cover art by Ao Nekonabe

This book is a work of fiction. Names, characters, places, and incidents are the product of the author's imagination or are used fictitiously. Any resemblance to actual events, locales, or persons, living or dead, is coincidental.

KIMI TO BOKU NO SAIGO NO SENJO, ARUIWA SEKAI GA HAJIMARU SEISEN Vol.4
©Kei Sazane, Ao Nekonabe 2018
First published in Japan in 2018 by KADOKAWA CORPORATION, Tokyo.
English translation rights arranged with KADOKAWA CORPORATION, Tokyo, through TUTTLE-MORI AGENCY, INC., Tokyo.

English translation © 2020 by Yen Press, LLC

Yen Press, LLC supports the right to free expression and the value of copyright. The purpose of copyright is to encourage writers and artists to produce the creative works that enrich our culture.

The scanning, uploading, and distribution of this book without permission is a theft of the author's intellectual property. If you would like permission to use material from the book (other than for review purposes), please contact the publisher. Thank you for your support of the author's rights.

Yen On
150 West 30th Street, 19th Floor
New York, NY 10001

Visit us at yenpress.com
facebook.com/yenpress
twitter.com/yenpress
yenpress.tumblr.com
instagram.com/yenpress

First Yen On Edition: September 2020

Yen On is an imprint of Yen Press, LLC.
The Yen On name and logo are trademarks of Yen Press, LLC.

The publisher is not responsible for websites (or their content) that are not owned by the publisher.

Cataloging in Publication data is on file with the Library of Congress.

ISBNs: 978-1-9753-0577-2 (paperback)
       978-1-9753-0578-9 (ebook)

10 9 8 7 6 5 4 3 2 1

LSC-C

Printed in the United States of America

Our Last Crusade
OR THE RISE OF A
New World

So Se lu, Ez shela noi xel.
A prayer to the planet.

corna, soo, vayne, loar, lue, flow. Ahw neo evoia faite ria xel.
Fire and water, earth and wind, sound and light, all are offerings to adorn this world.

Sew sia lukia Sec kamyu. Sera lu E lukia Ses qelno.
I will let you see my past if you show me the future.

PROLOGUE

Memories

"Saint Disciple Iska."

"Charged with treason for helping a witch break out of prison. Facing life in prison."

Turning back to a year prior, there was an incident where a witch captured by the largest nation in the world—known as the Empire—was saved by an Imperial swordsman.

The witch was fourteen at the time, a young girl with lingering naivete.

Nevertheless, the Empire had no mercy for witches.

She would be subjected to unspeakable torture.

But her rescue came on the eve of her day of judgment. It had been a sleepless night as she contemplated the terrifying fate that awaited her in the morning.

"Shhh. Keep quiet. I'm gonna let you out right now."

"Why? …Why are you…letting me escape…?"

* * *

Why would an Imperial soldier save a witch? What would he gain from this? Was this a trap?

The witch couldn't process the sudden developments, but she followed his instructions to escape.

She couldn't give up here.

She needed to *succeed in her mother's footsteps.*

Despite her dire situation, she eventually managed to slip away from Imperial territory and returned to her homeland of Nebulis after an arduous journey.

But…what welcomed the witch upon her homecoming wasn't relief but a new feeling of solitude.

…That's right.

…There's no one on my side, even in this country.

She started to remember everything after her fear of captivity subsided.

"…No!"

Before she could plunge into despair, the battered witch bit her lip and forced herself to run…all the way to the royal palace and into her dwelling—the dreaded castle where the worst of traitors made their nest.

"I refuse to hand the country over to those disloyal rogues. I will succeed my mother and become queen. Isn't that right, Sisbell?" she asked herself.

She was Sisbell Lou Nebulis IX, the youngest of three princesses and one of those with a claim to the throne.

It would take a few more days before she learned the Imperial soldier's name: Iska.

At present, fate was ready to bring the witch and swordsman together again, gently guided by the planet's mischief.

CHAPTER 1

Off to Vacation

1

"Iska! Over here! C'mon! Pick up the pace!"

"H-hey, Captain Mismis, what are you doing?! I'll wait over here so please go ahead with Nene!"

"It'll be fine. You're just tagging along with some girls on a little shopping trip. Doesn't that sound like fun?"

"You've got to be kidding me!"

Yunmelngen, capital of the Empire, the largest nation in the world, backed by the most militant army to ever walk the earth.

In a shopping mall built in the business zone, Iska had been apprehended by Captain Mismis, who now dragged him down its aisles.

"Look at your little red face! You're overreacting, Iska. We're only picking out some clothes together."

"...I'd really rather not." He sulked, yanked around by his captain, who showed no signs of easing up.

Iska would be seventeen this year. He had dark-brown hair.

He was part of the Special Defense Third Division in the military, which meant he had a duty to protect the populace from the witches of the Nebulis Sovereignty, the Empire's greatest enemy.

...At least, that was what he should've been doing...instead, they were at the mall.

"Every fiber in my body and soul is crying out for a vacation, Iska!" The petite captain whirled around, clenching her fist.

Captain Mismis Klass was more than a whole head smaller than Iska and sported a friendly face. She looked exactly like a child despite being a grown woman at twenty-two.

"We risk our lives fighting every day! Sometimes you've just gotta put your duties on hold and give your mind a break. Right?"

"Sure."

"In that case, it's your duty to accompany your captain on her vacation!"

"What about *my* plans?! I'd like to forget my responsibilities and take it easy, too."

"Oh, that's not very mature, Iska. As a member of society, you shouldn't forget your place in life. You're under my supervision around the clock, even on your time off. Heh-heh." Mismis looked at Iska with glee.

As the captain mentioned, they were in the middle of a long holiday—sixty days off. Iska had never had a break that long.

"Iska, come on! Nene is waiting for us."

"..."

"It's been a while since I've worn one of these! I'm so excited! What kind of pattern should I go for? What do you think, Iska?"

"...I don't even know what to say," he offered meekly, looking down in embarrassment.

Every other customer was a woman. Because he was a boy, Iska stuck out like a sore thumb as the only male. Everyone was shooting daggers at him.

"Whoa! Get a load of this, Iska. This swimsuit is so scandalous! I mean, it's basically just a few strings!"

They were in the section for women's swimsuits.

Mismis was browsing through the overflowing racks, pointing out the best ones in amusement. As for Iska, he couldn't even raise his head.

The stares from the other customers were so painful.

Iska was the only man in this section of the store.

Why is he in this store? He felt he could hear their internal monologue.

"You were all for it at first. What happened?"

"You told me we were going shopping. I had no idea you were talking about swimsuits…"

"Hee-hee. Oh, come on."

His superior picked up a leopard-print swimsuit that was very mature. It was as if she was intentionally trying to draw his attention.

"Iska, be honest."

"…About what?"

"That seeing me in a swimsuit makes you the happiest man in the world."

"Nuh-uh."

"So do you like this one or the one with the strings? Hmm? Neither? You're so bold, Iska! Hee-hee. What's a girl to do?"

"…As long as you're enjoying yourself, Captain." Iska heaved out a sigh as she continued to browse the store in high spirits.

Why was he here?

For starters, it was strange that headquarters had *ordered* them to take a long vacation.

But there was one thing he knew for certain: They needed to use this vacation to allow Captain Mismis to leave the capital as soon as possible.

In her current state, she was an enemy of the Empire…because she had become a witch—one who brings calamity onto the Empire.

It had all gone down ten days ago.

Right after Iska had escaped from the Paradise of Witches and the clutches of Alice the Ice Calamity Witch, making his return to the Empire.

2

The Heavenly Empire. The unified stronghold. Also known as the Empire for short.

Lauded as a mechanical utopia, the country had the greatest military in the world, backed by an expertise in machinery that lent itself to weapons development.

Was war the goal of the army?

Headquarters would answer *no* to this hypothetical question.

Its purpose was simply to purge the world of witches and sorcerers.

Ultimately, they claimed their reason for being was to protect humanity. For the sake of their mission, the military grew by the day.

At the gate from the military zone in the central capital…

"Test subject: Iska.

"The physician has finished a full-body examination and evaluated

CHAPTER 1

any risks for contamination. The psychiatrist has analyzed his mental state. All clear."

Psssh. The door to the classified room opened in the military medical center.

"The inspection is complete. Please make your way outside," instructed a woman's voice from the ceiling.

It was monotone, as if a machine were using human voices to speak.

"Thank you for your service. You have been granted permission to enter the capital."

"...Are you going to tell me the results of the examination?"

"The institution has already notified headquarters."

Meaning he didn't have the clearance to hear the report.

Iska noted this, nodding with a pained smile. "And the others?"

"We have found nothing unusual with Captain Mismis or the other two individuals. Please join them in the first-floor lobby."

"Okay... Thanks."

He changed from the white medical gown into his fairly worn combat uniform before following the instructions to head to the lobby. Three familiar faces were waiting for him.

"Hey, Iska's back! They said I was fine!"

Nene was the first one to call out, trotting over to him as her voluminous red ponytail swayed behind her.

She was their communications engineer and already recognized as a top-tier mechanic at fifteen years old.

"Nothing went wrong with the exam, right? Right?" Nene pressed.

"Obviously."

"Thank goodness." Nene calmed her racing heart.

That seemed dramatic, but even Iska had been tense as he was waiting to hear his results.

...Of course the government would be suspicious about whether I came back in "one piece"...even though I'm an Imperial soldier who's made it out alive from a hostage situation in the Sovereignty.

The Nebulis Sovereignty. The Paradise of Witches.

Just days before, Iska had been captive as their prisoner.

"I'll defeat him.

"In exchange—as the condition for my release—you must promise that you won't interfere while my unit and I return to the border."

They had passed the Sovereign border and reached an Imperial airbase by traveling through a few neutral cities. Once aboard air transport, they had managed to return home eight hours ago.

Did that mean everything was settled?

Well, headquarters gave them all orders to undergo physical examinations—essentially, health checks.

"What did they examine, Nene?"

"Um, just this—to observe how my mark has been changing."

Nene stretched out her arm as though she was looking at a wristwatch. A faint red mark pulsed on the back of her hand.

It was an astral crest, the mark of a witch possessed by astral power.

If this had been a real one, Nene would have been apprehended on the spot.

"I think yours is starting to disappear, Nene."

"Yeah, Risya said it'd last a week at most."

Nene's crest was fake, like an artificial tan. She had been irradiated with a small amount of astral energy, which caused this mark to appear on her skin.

CHAPTER 1

...Brief exposure isn't enough to possess anyone with astral power... which is why she hasn't become a witch. That's their logic.

Iska had a vague understanding of the theory, but he couldn't even imagine the technology that could make this happen.

"What about you, Jhin?"

"Mine hasn't changed yet. Seems there are slight individual differences."

Jhin was the sniper sitting in one of the chairs, lazily leaning onto its backrest.

He was a year older than Iska at eighteen, a young man with silver hair that stuck straight up, sharp gray eyes, and a tough face. He wore a gray combat uniform and kept a case carrying his sniper rifle tucked under his arm.

His artificial crest should have been on his ankle, which was hidden by his shoe.

"Mine is already concealed, but you should wear gloves or something, Nene. Things could get annoying if some soldiers witnessed it without knowing about our special mission," Jhin said.

"O-okay."

"Twelve other units were subjected to astral power. That's fifty-one people. Ninety-nine percent of the Imperial Army has no idea what's been going on."

"I'm having all four of you infiltrate the Nebulis Sovereignty undetected.

"Your special mission is to infiltrate the Sovereignty. Then capture the current Nebulis queen."

The Saint Disciple Risya had ordered them to execute this operation: They would need to get past the Sovereign checkpoints with their artificial crests and pull off a top secret mission to kidnap the queen of witches.

...Our unit is back...but I imagine the other eleven units are lying low and waiting for their opportunity to strike.

Most Imperial soldiers didn't even know a single detail about the special mission, which meant Iska's unit needed to make sure they didn't let anyone see their crests.

"And? Iska, what about you?"

"Me?"

"Your exam took the longest. I imagine they were thorough for your investigation, huh."

"Nope, just the usual. I was checked by a physician and a psychiatrist. And then they checked if I'd been contaminated by anything in the Sovereignty. They also took an X-ray to check whether their government hid anything in my body."

An Imperial soldier had come home after being imprisoned.

That wasn't always a joyous thing. After all, the soldier could have been "remodeled" by the hands of the witches.

"And they examined me for astral energy."

"Really? But they didn't give you an artificial crest. You wouldn't test positive for astral energy," Nene pointed out.

"You can be brainwashed into possessing it, but it's a really rare skill."

Astral power could manipulate a person's mind.

Iska could have been affected by these mind-controlling tactics while he was in Nebulis, locked away in the land of the witches. The government had to investigate him to cover all their bases.

"They also kept pestering me about whether I'd been tortured or interrogated."

"What did you tell them?" Nene asked.

CHAPTER 1

"Exactly what I told you. Since I was taken away while on a sedative, they couldn't do anything to me until I woke up."

A half-truth.

He hadn't been tortured or threatened. That much was true. Though he'd been in handcuffs, Iska had been put up in the penthouse suite of a hotel without a want in the world…with Alice, the princess of the enemy nation.

"I'll watch you personally from now on. Think of it as a privilege."

If there was one lie in Iska's testimony, it was in the part that nothing had happened.

Even headquarters wouldn't have imagined that Iska and the Ice Calamity Witch had witnessed each other's real faces on the battlefield.

…Not that they would believe me if I told them.

…Even if I let it slip, they'd suspect I'm a Sovereign spy.

After all, he had been the one to help a witch break out of prison a year ago, which had caused him to lose his title as a Saint Disciple.

Iska felt guilty for lying to Jhin and Nene, but he was afraid this knowledge would put his companions in danger of getting charged for conspiracy.

And if he was to tack on one more thing…

"…Well…could you do something about your clothes soon? Or at least put on some underwear?"

"Ahhh?! I-Iska! You're shameless! Where do you think you're staring?!"

"You're the one who came out to show yourself off, Alice!"

*   *   *

It would be better to not go there.

Alice had come stark naked out of the bath, which had been too much for a boy of his impressionable age. Just thinking about it was enough to make him blush.

...I'll forget it ever happened. I have to forget. I need to.

...Or I'll never be able to sleep again.

"Iska? Your face is red," Nene observed.

"I-it's nothing. I'm fine! ...I should have addressed this sooner, but..."

Behind Jhin, a sleeping girl with blue hair was sprawled over the waiting chairs. Well, she wasn't technically a girl. She'd be mad if she was treated like a child.

From her posture, everyone would think she was a cute kid, though she was a full-blown adult.

"What are you doing, Captain Mismis?"

"..."

"Captain?"

"An escapist tactic," Jhin answered for her, turning to the seats behind him and jerking his chin in her direction. She continued concealing her left shoulder as she slept. "Hey, wake up, boss. They just need to check your crest again. So what? You still have a whole week until your next appointment."

"Aaaah?! Stop! Don't talk about it!" The captain sprang up from her seat. "Oh, Iska, Iska, Iska. Your time has come. I risked my life to rescue you from the Sovereignty. It's your turn to come save me!"

"Calm down, Captain. What's gotten into you? Did they find something in your exam?" Iska asked, even though he knew the announcement had told him they hadn't found anything in the four of them.

CHAPTER 1

"No, but we're all getting inspected again," Nene said.

"Why?"

"Well, because our astral crests haven't disappeared yet," she explained, stroking her prided ponytail. "They said we're getting exams until the astral crests go away. That's why we have to come back in a week."

"...Huh."

Their skin should have returned to its original state after a short time, like a sunburn. At the longest, these artificial crests made by a special technique should have lasted one week. After that, the astral energy would dissolve and disappear from the skin.

"I know my mark and Nene's will definitely be gone by then. Our next appointment will just confirm that. The real issue is the boss's—"

"Stop! Don't say another word, Jhin!" begged Captain Mismis, clutching his back to stop him from finishing his sentence. "If someone hears you..."

"I wasn't going to say it. Not in this stupid facility," Jhin whispered.

It wasn't like he could speak the truth.

Unlike the other two marks, Captain Mismis's astral crest on her left shoulder was real.

She had become a witch.

Because she had fallen into a vortex, which was the eruption of astral energy, Captain Mismis had been possessed by astral power.

...Even though Jhin's and Nene's crests will eventually disappear, Captain Mismis's is here to stay.

...In other words, they'll find out it's real during the next exam.

It wasn't difficult to conceal a crest to the eye. A skin-colored bandage usually did the trick. Or even surgical tapes to hide skin lesions.

"But the real issue is astral energy leaking out of the bruise. You can't hide that with a bandage. Specialized machinery will detect it."

"...Wh-what should I do?"

"Calm down, boss. Nothing about our situation has changed with this mission. We needed to find a plan for the astral crest anyway. Now we just have a concrete deadline. A week."

"...And if we can't figure anything out?"

"Just leave it to us," Jhin assured the timid captain looking at him imploringly. The sniper with silver hair didn't miss a beat as he nodded. "We'll get you out of the capital before you're caught. We should look into escape routes."

"Jhin, could you *please* take this seriously?"

"I'm dead serious. And don't talk so loudly. If somebody hears your voice— Huh?"

Clack... There was a footstep.

Two women appeared at the entrance of the medical center. One of them was wearing the uniform for the Imperial Army, and the other wore a black suit.

"That's illegal, Risya. I'll have to report this incident to the Imperial Senate."

"I saaaid I'm sorry, Mickey! I was in the wrong. Okay?"

"It's Michaela. Please refer to me by my full name when we're on the job."

"Senior Doctor of the United Medical Team at HQ Mickey."

"My full *name*, not my full title. Never mind. Pick up the pace."

"Ow! Ow!" yelped the petite woman, yanked forward by the taller one.

Iska knew one of them. This was his first time seeing the other person.

CHAPTER 1

"Oh, Risya!"

"Well, well, well... Mismis, glad to see you in good spirits." The Saint Disciple managed to wave, remaining slumped over.

Risya In Empire.

Her face was shrewd and graceful, accenting the black-rimmed glasses that made her look smart. On her slim and tall stature, even a normal combat uniform looked put together. Iska was shaken up to see her make an appearance at the outskirts of the Empire.

After all, she was the Saint Disciple in the fifth seat, meaning she didn't go too far from the throne, except on missions, as an officer who reported directly to the ruler. In any normal situation, she wouldn't be here but in the Imperial capital.

"What're you doing here, Risya?" Mismis asked.

"Oh... Well, you know. Ha-ha-ha..."

"Don't play stupid, Risya," warned the woman in the suit, grabbing Risya's hand. "It's nice to meet you, Unit 907. My name is Michaela." She bowed. "I work in the headquarters supervising medical teams. My specialty is in legal medicine, and I lead other teams related to medicine as part of my duties."

A medical officer. A soldier with special skills who served in the Imperial military and held a medical license.

...If she works in the headquarters...she must be in a higher rank than Captain Mismis.

Headquarters had a hierarchical structure from the First Division to the Sixth Division. If she was working for them, she must have ranked high despite her age.

"N-nice to meet you. Uh, um, did we do something wrong?" Mismis asked.

"We have a terrible problem."

"Wh-what is it?!"

There was no way... Could they have found out that the

captain had become a witch after she fell into the vortex? Her face paled. She was practically an open book.

"Risya needs to apologize for something."

"...Excuse me?"

"Headquarters manages battles engaged by all Imperial armies. In particular, legal medicine makes medical recommendations to optimize swift recovery."

"...I see. And?"

"I checked all your service records."

They must have been stored in the clipboard tucked under her arm. Dr. Michaela flipped through bundles of printed papers.

"We recognize you've all worked overtime. According to military law, the Third Division can engage in battle for a maximum of thirty consecutive days. In emergency conditions, an extension to forty-five days can be granted. We do not only count actual combat. We include practices that require an equal amount of physical exertion. We can see you've all clearly exceeded the limits and—"

"Wait. The boss isn't following your explanation." Jhin patted Mismis on the back as her mind drifted off into space. "Please summarize."

"You're *overworked*." The physician held up a paper covered in red circles. "And it's in violation of the regulations."

"What?! B-but we were ordered to deploy."

"Exactly. The onus is on your superior. This person." Michaela pointed at Risya, who was looking away. "Isn't that right, Risya?"

"...Well...it was only a little."

"A little what?"

"L-listen, I said I'm sorry, all right?! It was all my fault. Don't look at me like that!" Risya seemed uncomfortable, offering a dry smile. "It was necessary for the Empire. What else was I supposed to do?"

CHAPTER 1

"There are other elite units in the military. We'll be decried by the populace if we abuse a single unit to the point they can't work anymore." The doctor pointed at Risya's chest with the clipboard. "After their battle with the Ice Calamity Witch, you ordered them to search for the vortex immediately. Right? Both orders were after purebreds. *Right?*"

"...W-well, yeah."

"Which is the same as *sending them to their deaths. Twice.* If they were a normal unit."

An edge of the clipboard poked Risya in the chest.

"It all comes down to the special mission to capture the queen of Nebulis. Just four days after the search for the vortex, you dispatched Unit 907 to the border! Three dangerous areas in less than two months. That's just too much."

"..."

"Three times, they've almost been annihilated! Word hasn't spread because there have been no victims, but if the other units find out, they could question if headquarters can make sound judgments."

"It's all good. As long as we don't get caught, right?"

"It's! A! Huge! Problem!" Michaela barked, brow furrowed. "Risya. You're not taking this seriously. It doesn't matter if you're a Saint Disciple, which affords you a slightly high position. This is what headquarters has decided. Even I can't let this slide as your friend. If you didn't have connections in legal medicine, you wouldn't even be able to get that *drug*—"

"Okay, Mickey. That's enough."

"Nh!"

Risya had placed a fingertip over the doctor's lips. Dr. Michaela turned red, bewitched by this surprising move.

"Anyhoo, sorry!" The Saint Disciple put her hands together

in apology and bowed her head. "I was surprised when Mickey pointed this out to me. I never would have guessed you were overworked! Imagine my surprise."

"Risya, you're terrible!" Captain Mismis squawked back, unable to bottle it up anymore. "I had a feeling your demands were unreasonable! I can't believe these were all according to your whims! Thanks to that whole vortex incident, I'm a—"

"Boss."

"Oh— Yow?! Aha-ha-ha-ha... N-never mind." Mismis went quiet for a moment after Jhin kicked her in the rear. "S-so what are we supposed to do?"

"Follow regulations." Michaela immediately stopped blushing and cleared her throat. "In the event that a soldier exceeds the maximum for consecutive combat, you are granted a special work leave to encourage rest and recuperation. I believe you would receive a sixty-day holiday at minimum."

"Sixty days?!"

"Let me repeat that Risya's orders would have killed you all three times. The medical team judged that any more combat will place you in danger."

The papers in her clipboard notified them of these decisions.

Michaela handed the documents signed by headquarters over to Captain Mismis.

"Unit 907, you have been ordered to go on special leave for sixty days. This has been decided by headquarters. It supersedes all orders except those directly given by the throne. We will give you notice of more details sometime today, but if you have any questions, you may ask them now."

"I have one," Jhin said.

"Go ahead."

"Why are you 'ordering' this? Usually, you would 'grant' it to us."

CHAPTER 1

"Excellent question." Dr. Michaela nodded and smiled cryptically at Risya next to her. "This isn't a privilege but a command. We're not telling you that you *may* take a break—we're *ordering* you to take one."

"Meaning?"

"For the next sixty days, you are forbidden from participating in any voluntary training or practices. Even if a *certain* Saint Disciple tries to coerce Mismis into working because she's bored on break." The doctor looked pointedly at Risya, who was staring in another direction. "I know it can be difficult to turn down a Saint Disciple's request. I imagine one of them might ask you to participate in 'independent study sessions' or 'hang out,' which just happens to be more training."

"Seems likely. A favorite trick of a certain Saint Disciple," Jhin agreed.

"To prevent that, we're ordering you to take time off."

A sixty-day compulsory leave.

During that time, they could ignore all orders.

"It would be best if you went somewhere far away. Somewhere outside the capital. Or even beyond our borders. Then even she wouldn't be able to proposition you to do more things. How would you feel about resting in an ally nation on the outskirts of the Empire?"

"But we've been told to be on standby for another exam in a week."

"That has been postponed."

"—"

Jhin and Nene nodded just the tiniest bit. The doctor mustn't have caught Captain Mismis's eyes glittering with hope.

"I know the situation surrounding the astral crests, which means headquarters understands, too. We've already done enough sample tests to know they'll disappear in a week. We can wait to reexamine you until you've returned to the capital, though I imagine your astral crests will be gone by then."

"Uh-huh. Right, boss?"

"What?! Ah, right!" Mismis nodded over and over.

"That's all there is to say. We're going back, Risya. We have work to do."

"Mickey, I'd like some time off, too."

"You're a Saint Disciple, which means you're out of the jurisdiction of headquarters. Please discuss that with the throne."

"Aw, come on! …Ugh. Bye, guys. Enjoy your vacation. 'Cause I'm gonna work you to the bone when you get back!" shouted the Saint Disciple as she was dragged out of the lobby.

They were alone again.

"Erm?" hesitantly started the girl with the ponytail. "That means we've been saved, right? Now Captain Mismis has some time until—"

"Neeeeeene!"

"Whoa?!" Nene staggered when the tiny captain pounced on her.

"Yay! We're on break! We don't have to worry about Risya's unreasonable demands, *and* we can postpone our next appointment! This is awesome!"

"This is not 'awesome.' Context clues." Jhin leaned back in a chair again and looked up at the ceiling. "It's what that doc just said. Those three expeditions all could have annihilated a normal unit. We were at death's door this whole time. Headquarters is implying that *just sixty days of special leave is adequate exchange for our experiences.*"

They had repeatedly sent a single unit to the verge of death.

Their compensation was a measly sixty days of special leave

written off as recuperation. Jhin was right: It was a reward that didn't suit the reality of the situation.

...And if I take it a step further...I imagine they're going to send us out into harm's way in sixty days.

Of course, Iska had guessed that, too. But the difference between the two boys was that one of them would stay silent about this revelation and the other wouldn't.

"It's true we escaped death by a hair," Jhin said.

"R-right! And our deadline has changed from a week to sixty days! It's going to be a piece of cake!" Captain Mismis nodded. Her voice was filled with spirit, which was totally different from just minutes earlier. "Okay! ...Um, Iska, what should we do?"

"Let's get out of the Empire. We need to leave the capital at least. Pretend we're going on a trip."

There were traps to capture witches in the streets within the capital—to detect astral energy. As military personnel, Iska's unit knew their general placements. If Mismis entered those spaces, the traps would immediately activate.

...From the streets, to public bathhouses, to grocery store doors... The capital is packed with detectors.

At present, Mismis had been staying put in the women's barracks, while Nene had been going out to shop in her place. If this kept up for too long, people would start suspecting something.

"I agree!" Nene said. "The capital is dangerous. It'd look more natural for us to pretend we're going on vacation. I think we should return in exactly sixty days. I guess all that's left is figuring out where we're going... Ummm, opinions?" Nene asked.

"...Maybe a neutral city?" Iska suggested.

"No way!" Nene cried.

"Rejected," warned Jhin.

"Do you even hear yourself, Iska?" Mismis yelped.

His idea was viciously turned down.

"Iska, haven't you reflected on what happened?" Nene asked.

"You were *just* carried off to the Nebulis Sovereignty when a certain person poisoned you in a neutral city."

"That was such an ordeal."

"...I—I said I was sorry! That wasn't why I suggested it... Hey!" Iska waved his hands to dispel their distrust as they continued to glare at him.

The three of them were convinced that Iska had been kidnapped because of the brutality of the Ice Calamity Witch. He alone knew that Alice hadn't meant to do anything.

"I-it's not what you think! I didn't want this!

"I didn't mean for this to happen at all! Rin did it on her own without me!"

This hadn't been Alice's plan.

She exploded at her attendant, Rin, to ensure the incident wouldn't be repeated, which he knew about. That was why Iska had let his mouth slip by suggesting the neutral city.

...Right. Jhin, Nene, and Mismis...all consider the neutral cities unsafe.

If Iska tried to head over to one, they were sure to object, which meant he wouldn't be able to go to the neutral cities anymore.

In other words, he wouldn't have any more chances to "accidentally" run into Alice.

That meant he would actually need to stumble across her... somewhere in this expansive world or on a distant battlefield... It could take years... Even if he offered his entire life, it was a coincidence that might never be realized.

...What am I doing?

CHAPTER 1

…There isn't the time for that. I need to think about what I can do to save the captain.

They would head out of the capital, but not to a neutral city.

"We could go to one of the Imperial allies like Dr. Michaela just suggested. Or an independent nation, which could be far."

"Which would you prefer, Iska?" asked Mismis.

"The latter. I think it'd be safer to go to a place that isn't an ally."

The allies were a group of countries that openly cooperated with the Imperial Army. They weren't anti-witch enough to declare war on the Nebulis Sovereignty, but their defense industry did export a substantial amount of energy to the Empire.

"I think it'd be possible for headquarters to surveil us there," Iska said.

"…You're right."

He sighed.

Captain Mismis folded her arms, speaking in muted tones. "We should try going somewhere with as few ties to the Empire as possible. And it has to be a place far from Nebulis. And a known vacation spot…"

"I'll look into it!" Nene raised her hand immediately. "We just went to that casino, so I think we should find someplace in the south! I wanna go to a resort with huge beaches and pools! What about you, Captain?"

"A place where we can all have a barbecue together."

"And what about you, Jhin?" Nene asked.

"Nothing in particular."

"All right. And you, Iska?"

Did he have any requests?

Iska stared at the ceiling for a few beats while the girl with the ponytail looked at him expectantly.

"Nothing from me, too. Let's prepare to leave as soon as possible."

They would leave the capital. That was their highest priority.

This "mechanical utopia" was no paradise for a witch like Mismis.

And that was how they had come to the present.

Iska continued to gape at the swimsuit section of a shopping mall in the capital.

...Something is off. Something is definitely weird.

...We were taking this so seriously yesterday... Why am I here?

Why was he looking at swimsuits in the women's section? Everyone else was a young woman. It was weird that Iska was mingling among this crowd.

Was he like a wolf hiding among a flock of sheep? Not quite.

If anything, Iska was the sheep surrounded by a pack of wolves.

"Iska, over here!"

He heard Nene call out from the back of the store.

She had poked her head out of the curtain to the changing room, which was fine, except he could see a sliver of her pale skin from beyond.

Of course, she wasn't wearing underwear, much less any clothes.

Her thin torso and navel were bare for all to see...

"Nene! Your clothes!"

"I had to take them off. I'm trying on swimsuits. Hey, what do you think of this?"

The girl with the ponytail pulled the curtain open and leaped out of the changing room. She was in a red halter top that was very exposing.

Nene was born with the long limbs of a model, though she looked more like a fit athlete from days of intense training. Her taut stomach and curvy thighs were silky smooth.

"Heh-heh. How's that? I bet this is enough to make even you horny, Iska."

"...'Horny'? Where'd you learn that?"

It was obvious Nene had matured over the past year or two. Iska almost eyed this change for too long, but he managed to shake his head in a fluster.

That wouldn't be good. This was the women's swimsuit section. He couldn't look *too* closely at a girl in a swimsuit. What would the other customers think?

"...It's cute, but don't you think it's a bit too risqué, Nene?"

"You think so? It might be a little too mature for me. Hmm, then maybe I'll go with this one. But I don't really want to rule out this one, either."

"Nene, it's great that you're choosing a swimsuit, but..."

Though he had scruples about throwing water on her fun, he couldn't let her get carried away. They weren't going to the resort to have fun, after all.

"We're going to escape the capital, and I'm sure Captain Mismis is taking this seriously—"

"You called?"

Someone poked him in the back.

Iska turned around to find Captain Mismis holding a gigantic paper bag in both her hands.

"...Captain, what's with those sunglasses?"

"Hmm? We're going on vacation, silly. If a proper adult woman will be traipsing around beaches, sunglasses are in order."

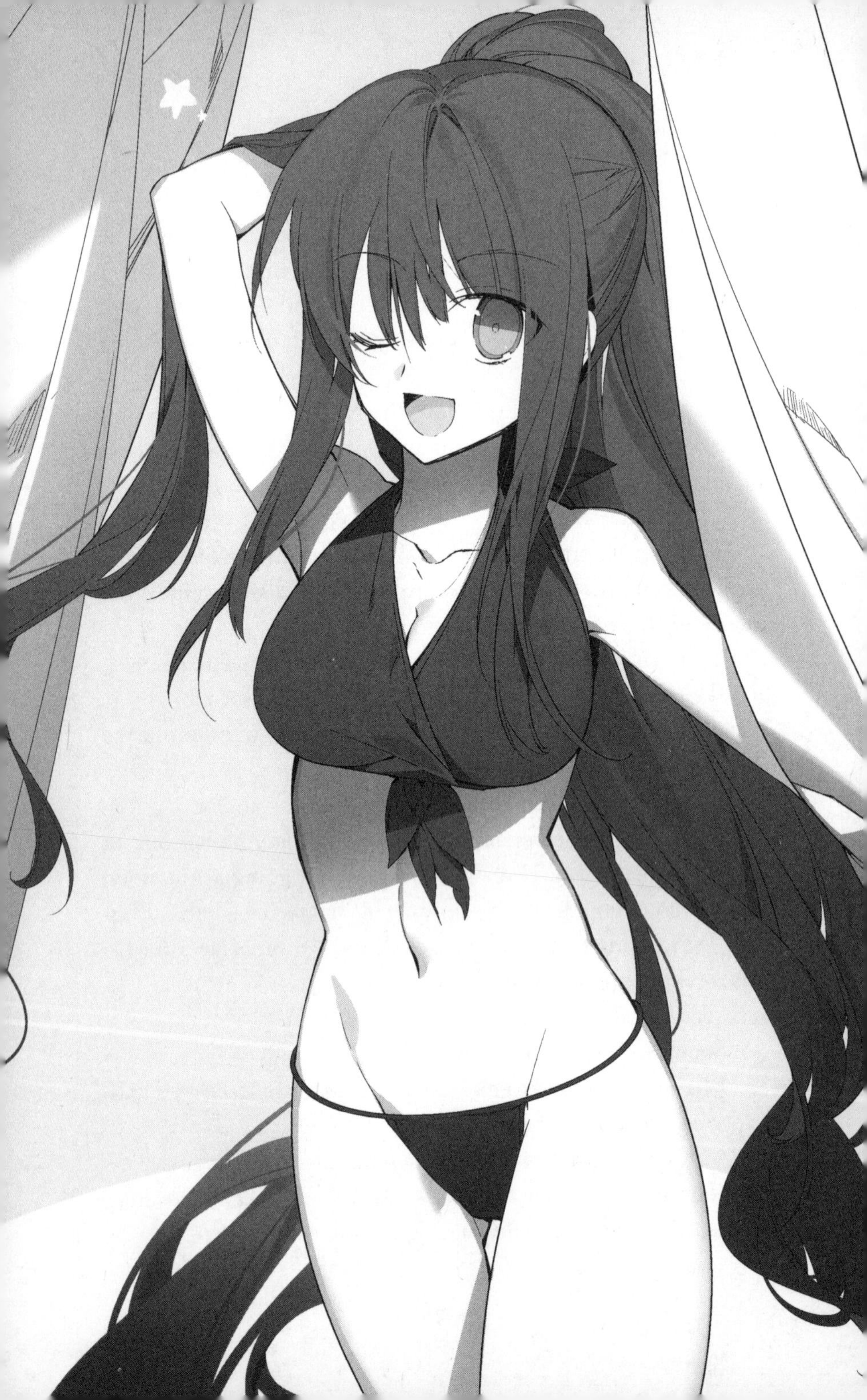

CHAPTER 1

A pair of flashy sunglasses was perched on her baby face. They really didn't look good on her at all.

She had a child's floating device over her shoulders and a large sun hat balanced on her head. Every piece of her outfit clashed.

"You look like a kid who got tricked by a fashion magazine into wearing the latest trends..."

"H-hey!" The captain clutched the paper bag in both her hands. "Hee-hee, I've already picked out my swimsuit. I can't wait to go to a luxury resort far from the Empire—surrounded by nothing but desert! I've always wanted to go!"

"...Glad to see you having fun, Captain."

Even her skin was glowing. Just the other day, she'd been pale, as though they were at the end of the world. But right now, she smiled, as if she didn't have a care in the world.

...She said Nene showed her the brochure for the resort last night... and that's what made a difference.

Or was she just putting on a brave face? Iska had contemplated this possibility until they'd arrived at the mall, but it seemed she really had cheered up considerably.

"It's your first time at the independent state of Alsamira, right, Iska?" Captain Mismis asked, looking up at the ceiling from her sunglasses. "It was created in an oasis in a huge desert east of the Empire. I heard the entire country is basically a resort. You can swim in a pool during the sunrise! And at night, you lie in the desert and sleep under the stars. How romantic...!"

"And we're leaving tonight."

"Yup. Jhin made a reservation for the bus. We're gonna transfer to get there," Mismis said.

They were going out of Imperial territory from the capital, and they would go by way of a neutral city and head to a far-east desert. It would take over three days to travel there one-way.

"I let Jhin handle all the formalities. Do you think he's okay? Apparently, the request for a special leave is more trouble than I thought," Mismis said.

"Jhin will be fine."

He had stayed behind in the Imperial base as Iska escorted Nene and Mismis.

But Iska knew the truth: Jhin had volunteered to shoulder this responsibility because he hadn't wanted to pick out swimsuits with the captain.

"…That was unfair, Jhin," Iska complained to himself.

"What's wrong, Iska?" asked Nene.

"Nothing. We should hurry back and pack."

Iska could feel the icy glares of the employees on him as he turned tail and ran out of there.

3

A century prior, the Empire had been extolled for dominating the world using military force even greater than its present army. It took over other nations, giving rise to its glory.

But one day, the Empire stumbled upon a planetary secret: astral power, an almost impossible source of energy that had seeped out of the planet's core.

As it broke through the surface, it began to possess humans, bequeathing them with powers out of magical fairy tales. They became more powerful than weapons of mass destruction, and the Imperial populace began to fear them, labeling them as witches and sorcerers. That was when the persecution had begun, making way for an era of witch hunts…until a certain witch bared her fangs at the Empire that had used excessive force to oppress them.

CHAPTER 1

This started the rebellion of the Grand Witch Nebulis. She had been in only her teens when she founded the Nebulis Sovereignty, which would become a nation with power rivaling the Empire.

The Empire was trying to eliminate all witches and sorcerers.

The Nebulis Sovereignty blazed with feelings of revenge.

The war between the two greatest nations of the world showed no sign of abating, even a century later.

The sunset pierced into the Star Spire of the palace in Nebulis.

In the small room used for official duties, not a single footstep could be heard.

Even the noise of dust filtering through the air seemed loud. The only detectable sound was the quiet sweeps of a pen as a blond girl wrote in a frenzy.

"…" She glanced over a report and signed it.

Then she picked up another document to sign, which she continued to do for the next twenty documents before glancing at the edge of her desk.

"These are from two weeks ago."

Thud, echoed the mountain of documents dropped on her table.

"You'll be done after reviewing these reports and the ones from this week and last week, Lady Alice."

"Please have mercy!" Alice yelped, leaping out of her seat without meaning to.

Aliceliese Lou Nebulis IX. The second princess of the Paradise of Witches, known by its residents as the Nebulis Sovereignty.

Her silky golden hair was radiant. Her ruby eyes housed a certain air of sophistication. Though she was only seventeen, she had developed sensual curves early for her age, which made her captivating. Her body contained astral powers consistent with her status as the direct descendant of Nebulis.

She was the leading candidate to become the next queen, which afforded her a certain reputation.

Except she was close to backing up against a wall in the study and crying, *No more! No more!*

"I can't do this anymore. Look, Rin! Look at this calloused hand! I've been holding my pen for too long! This is the last of the work to assist the queen. Right?"

"But you have a whole other hand. That one can hold a pen, I'm sure."

"Do you *want* to torture me?"

"...Joking aside, how about we take a short break?" suggested Alice's attendant, Rin, carrying a bundle of paper in her arms.

Rin Vispose.

Her chestnut hair was parted evenly down the middle and tied into two bundles. She was one year younger than Alice.

Though she appeared to be in the dull uniform of a housekeeper, Rin had skillfully concealed daggers, metal needles, wires, and other instruments for assassination as Alice's guard.

"Hey, Rin. I'd like some tea. With lots of milk and sugar."

"I will have it prepared shortly."

In a learned manner, Rin spread out the tea set in the corner of the study.

Alice observed.

"...I'd like some excitement in my life," the princess muttered as she sat back down in her chair. "I've been holed up in this place all day helping Mother. This routine is making me drowsy. I wonder if there's any work more fitting for a princess."

"This is still part of your royal duties. Even if it's work behind the scenes."

CHAPTER 1

"But, Rin..."

"And didn't you get enough adrenaline the other day?"

"..." Alice took the hint. She didn't have anything else to say.

"Now you're under my watch!"

"Ha-ha, this could be fun from time to time. To have a powerful fighter from an enemy country attached to you. It's kind of exhilarating."

She felt she'd had a conversation like that when they had captured the Imperial soldier Iska and brought him to the Nebulis Sovereignty. That whole incident had happened only ten days ago.

Alice had been keeping watch over Iska as he was captive for days.

...I know this makes me a bad princess...but my heart raced when I was with him.

She had felt safe with Rin by her side, but there was a part of her that was excited and nervous to be around him, reminding herself to not let down her guard.

And she couldn't forget that pleasure.

...Plus...it was my first time sleeping in the same place with a boy of my age.

Alice was still a young girl, even though she was a princess. Even though Iska was a soldier from an enemy country, she was bound to feel something when they shared meals and conversations.

Alice had gotten a taste of excitement for the first time from eating and sleeping with Iska.

"You should have put that Imperial soldier in a cramped storehouse rather than the presidential suite. Then we wouldn't have had to worry about him attacking you in your sleep, Lady Alice."

"Rin," she gently warned her pouting attendant. "Iska wouldn't do that."

"..."

"You know that, right?"

"...I can't deny it." Rin's expression was dutiful. "That Imperial soldier is the enemy, but I imagine he can exercise reasonable discretion as a human. Even if he wasn't in handcuffs, I guess...he wouldn't have tried to attack you in your sleep."

"Right? I knew you'd come around."

On the battlefield, even Alice shivered from astonishment at his strength.

But outside of these arenas, Iska was an entirely different person—easygoing and demure without a discriminatory thought about witches, even though he was an Imperial soldier. He certainly seemed intelligent.

That was what made him so *great*.

If he had been rough and rowdy, Alice wouldn't have been as merciful to her captive.

"It's not as though I was being *compassionate* to an Imperial soldier. It's just that Iska is a special case."

"You almost had a panic attack when he saw you naked."

"Gah! ...I don't care! I'm not embarrassed of my body! If anything, I *wanted* to show him!"

"That's what a pervert would say!" Rin didn't even hide her sigh as she brought the tea set over. "Here's your milk tea. I've put in heaps of sugar. Stir it well before drinking."

"Thank you, Rin." Alice lifted the steaming cup, picking up the bitter notes of tea coming through the sweetness. "Hmm? I've never smelled this one before. Is it new?"

"Yes. We imported some tea from a distant region. A desert far to the east."

"They can make tea in the desert?" Alice asked.

CHAPTER 1

"Yes, at a farm on an oasis. The area is known for its resorts. I hear their tea is top-notch."

A desert oasis. A resort.

Something about those two phrases sounded very attractive to her.

"Hey, Rin! Let's go during our next break. I'm sure we can enjoy ourselves in a resort. We could swim to our hearts' content in a pool in the morning and lay out a towel in the desert to sleep under the stars. Isn't it romantic?"

"With your current schedule, the earliest opening is in two years."

"…So a far-off dream." Alice slumped back in her chair when she learned of the unforgiving situation.

That was when she heard fanfare from outside the spire.

It must have been coming from the courtyard. The palace filled with sounds of trumpets and brass instruments with a cadence that made all want to march with springing steps.

The people must have been able to hear it downtown, too.

"A fanfare marking a return. And this song is…"

"It must be my elder sister, Elletear."

This song was used to signal the return of the eldest of the three princesses of Nebulis.

Elletear, the eldest daughter.

Aliceliese, the middle child.

Sisbell, the youngest.

All three of them were mages born with rare astral powers and candidates to be the next queen.

They were siblings by blood.

But they would need to viciously fight one another in the conclave to select the next queen, even though they were sisters.

...For generations, the queen has given up her throne early... We have two years until my mother abdicates. Maybe three.

They would be a step behind if they waited until then to decide the next queen.

The fight for the throne was already brewing below the surface. This was especially true for Elletear. For the majority of the year, she traveled abroad without spending time in the castle.

The reason was for her to lay *groundwork*.

"She returned quickly this time. I wonder if that's an indication of favorable meetings with the electoral group for the throne."

"Rin," Alice scolded.

But it was true. While Alice was staying in the royal palace, her sister was visiting the nobles to bolster her support.

"Lady Elletear will be at the palace shortly. Would you like to welcome her, Lady Alice?"

"...Hmm. My heart isn't in it, but she *is* my sister."

Alice basically dragged her heavy legs as she headed out of the study, following her attendant.

"Oh!" Rin exclaimed when she opened the door.

Was there someone other than a soldier outside?

"What's the matter, Rin? Is it Elletear?" Alice peeked into the hallway from behind Rin.

Alice wasn't focusing on the beautiful first princess but the young and petite third princess.

"Sisbell?"

"..."

She had strawberry blond hair and an adorable face. Her large eyes reflected the light from the sun, glittering like jewels.

Her royal garb had a soft gradient that made her seem as though she were wearing something out of a fairy tale.

As her eyes bored into Alice, her gaze housed a certain

CHAPTER I

darkness. Alice wouldn't go so far as to call it hostility, but her sister was obviously vigilant.

"Sisbell, are you going to welcome our sister, too?"

"..."

"Perfect timing. Rin and I are going, too. Would you like to come with—?"

"Excuse me," Sisbell said curtly.

She turned on her heel and started walking down the hall before Alice could respond. She wasn't going to greet their sister. She was heading back to her room.

"It seems we caught her when she's out."

"Yes. That's just how she always acts...," Alice lamented.

Even Alice could see that her younger sister was as cute as a doll. When they were younger, she had been friendly and curious and boyish enough to rival Alice.

When had that changed?

When had Alice started to become frightened of Elletear and feel strange around Sisbell?

...Elletear is bright and lively and I like talking to her...but Sisbell is an enigma.

Alice couldn't guess what Sisbell was thinking.

Her sister holed herself up in her room, preferring not to show herself to anyone. She ate in her room most of the time, joining them at mealtime only if their mother invited her. Even when they happened to pass by each other in the hallway, she would immediately turn tail.

Was her sister scheming something unsavory?

"...Ugh!" Alice groaned, burying her face in her hands. "This is terrible. I'm gonna die from fatigue with both my sisters back. I just want to get out of the palace!"

Alice had come prepared with excuses.

There was that incident when the transcendental sorcerer, Salinger, had escaped from prison with the Imperial Army. How had the Saint Disciple Nameless's spies breached the country borders? Alice couldn't figure it out.

On top of that, the Imperial Army still might have been in hiding within the Sovereignty.

"What if I left to patrol the country from the outside?"

"No."

"Why not?!"

"It's a good option. Even the queen has suggested this. Too many of our best astral mages have gathered in the central state. We should be concerned about the Imperial Army making their next move."

"...Doesn't that mean I *should* go on a patrol?"

If the Ice Calamity Witch was to go out, it would cause the Imperial Army to proceed with caution. It would be effective for putting a check on any schemes to invade the border.

"It seems Sisbell is about to leave. She will depart the Sovereignty tomorrow."

"Really?" Alice doubted her ears. "I wonder if she was the one to suggest it."

"I heard it was ordered by the queen. She will tour through an independent nation to the east. It was a matter that could not be settled without Lady Sisbell's powers."

"...I see. They are very useful."

Sisbell Lou Nebulis IX's astral power was that of Illumination.

It did not suit direct battle, but there was no better ability when it came to information wars. It was powerful enough that she was feared by the retainers and soldiers in the royal palace.

"Which means you're minding the palace, Lady Alice. At least until Lady Sisbell is back."

CHAPTER 1

"..."

"Is that all you have to say?"

"...Fiiine."

Alice couldn't go against her mother's orders.

She planted her face on her desk in resignation.

The Imperial swordsman Iska must have already returned home. She wondered absentmindedly what he was doing at the moment.

"I need more adrenaline...," Alice mumbled to herself.

CHAPTER 2

Paradise and Shunning a Witch

1

The independent state of Alsamira. An oasis flourishing in a corner of the largest desert to the east of the continent.

Just like the neutral cities, it was affiliated with neither the Empire nor the Sovereignty, though Alsamira hadn't declared their neutrality. There was a chance the state would bend to the wishes of either country.

"I've heard the executives at headquarters have been trying to get them to side with the Empire under the table, according to some darker rumors. And it's been going on for decades."

"But they must have turned them down."

"Well, I mean, they've succeeded in making this a resort," explained Jhin to Iska as they looked out the window.

The loop bus slowly came to a halt.

After crossing the border to Alsamira, they would drive through the desert for an entire day and head to their destination, the urban area of the capital.

"Wow! This is amazing! Look at those giant buildings over there! They must all be hotels!"

Captain Mismis sounded delighted.

She pressed both her hands against the window, waiting expectantly for the bus to park in the lot.

"Don't head outside yet, Captain. You've got to wait for the bus to stop."

"Uh... Are we there yet? Are we there yet?" Mismis was hovering over her seat.

"Thank you for riding with us. We have finally arrived at the metropolis in Alsamira."

"I've been waiting for this!"

The doors opened at the exact moment Commander Mismis went tumbling right out of the bus. She carried a gigantic knapsack on her back, dressed to impress with her sun hat.

"It's scorching hot!"

That was the first thing out of the captain's mouth when she landed on the asphalt road.

"Wh-what's up with this heat? It hotter than summer... It's like being on top of a frying pan!"

"Obviously. You just came out of the air-conditioned bus."

Iska followed her, shouldering his luggage.

The captain was right. It felt like Iska had been blasted by an otherworldly heat wave when he stepped off the bus, blowing his hair around. He immediately started sweating bullets and could feel his lips drying up.

It must have been over a hundred degrees.

"Wow, this is something, huh, Jhin? It's summer year-round in this resort," Nene said.

"It *is* smack-dab in the middle of the desert."

CHAPTER 2

"It feels like…we're in another country. I can see palm trees in the distance! I guess the flora is different, since the climate is different." Nene looked around in wonder.

Meanwhile, Captain Mismis was rummaging in her bag.

"Here, Iska. Blow these up."

"What are they?"

"A pool float and a beach ball."

"You're jumping the gun! We've just gotten to the parking lot. We're nowhere near a pool! We can't go sightseeing until we check in and store our luggage at the hotel."

"Oh! Y-you're right…"

"All you've got is vacation on your mind."

They headed to the main road from the parking lot, where dozens of sightseeing buses and taxis had parked.

When they got there, tons of luxury hotels stood in a line.

"Hey, Iska! Look at that! The Mega-Marine Hotel! Hotel Isbelia! And Daikouha Hotels! They're all super famous. I feel like I'm dreaming!"

Captain Mismis was practically skipping as she ran down the main road lined with palm trees.

"Summer year-round! We've arrived in paradise at last. Let's go!"

"Captain! Please look where you're going when you—"

"Oh! Ow?!"

"I was trying to warn you, but I guess I didn't make it in time…"

She had collided at full force with a palm tree.

Iska, Jhin, and Nene exchanged glances as they watched the captain crouch on the ground after smacking her forehead.

2

Sand glittered on the beaches. It made a satisfying crunch under bare feet. Small bits of shell and coral must have mixed into the sand.

The tide was high for the most part, though the waves crashed softly on the beach.

"It's wonderful…"

It was hard to believe it was the hotel pool.

With sand imported from a distant ocean and a huge wave generator installed at the bottom, the pool even accommodated surfing.

Families could make full use of the small kiddie pool.

Young lovebirds were swimming in the lazy rivers or lying out to bake.

"Ahhh… This is agreeable." Iska nodded to himself alone at a corner of the crowded beach with tourists.

This was true paradise. A genuine resort.

He could understand why Captain Mismis was so excited. Even Iska could feel his heart beat faster just looking at the scene.

He could swim in any of the pools. Even a leisurely stroll on the beach would be nice. The fast-food places were stocked with drinks and snacks.

"Iska. Are Nene and the boss here yet?"

"Looks like they're still changing."

"Jeez. What's taking so long? The boss was the one who told us to change ASAP."

The person approaching him was a young man with silver hair.

Even Jhin had changed into an outfit for the pool, wearing a rash guard over his swimsuit like Iska instead of his usual battle uniform.

CHAPTER 2

Except Jhin's rash guard was bulging, because he had something hidden in there.

"Jhin, is that...?"

"A gun. All I could fit in my pocket was the smallest one on me," whispered the sniper to prevent anyone from hearing. His expression was dead serious.

The independent state of Alsamira did not prohibit the open carrying of a gun for self-defense with the proper identification. The only exception were guns that were very dangerous.

Regardless, weapons were strictly prohibited in the pool area.

"If they find out, they'll arrest you..."

"If I think they're on to me, I'll just toss it into the grass. I've got my usual sniper in the hotel anyway."

Jhin's favorite gun was camouflaged as a hunting rifle and currently in his room at the hotel.

"Can't know when a *civil war* might break out in this country."

Iska was the only one who had picked up on Jhin's comment.

If an Imperial soldier was to run into a witch, the weaponless soldier wouldn't have any way of fighting back against astral powers.

...You'd just be kidnapped to someplace out of the public eye and get beaten up... There wouldn't be an uproar. No one would even know it happened.

That was why they had defensive measures in place.

Though this place was a paradise, one had to be ready for whatever conflicts could occur below the water's surface.

"Well, the strategy is easy. We just need to make sure we aren't in the shopping areas after nightfall. Those witches wouldn't try pulling anything in the public eye."

"...Right."

"I'm more worried about having to hang out with those two." Jhin sighed.

The man with silver hair was looking toward the entrance to the pool, where Captain Mismis and Nene had their hands full carrying floating devices and beach balls, running toward the beach.

"There you are. I found you!" Nene exclaimed.

"Sorry for the holdup. It took a while to blow these up."

"..."

"What's wrong, Iska?" Nene asked.

"I—I mean, I should have expected you'd be in swimsuits. Um, obviously."

Under the sun, his two compatriots exposed their supple skin.

In her bathing suit, Nene seemed more radiant now than in the shopping mall at the capital. Maybe this was because they were on island time in this summer paradise.

"Hee-hee. What? Are you finally attracted to me?" Nene stooped down toward him.

Her frilly halter top made her limbs appear longer and slimmer than usual. Her chest and butt weren't as modest in size as he'd expected. He could see all her curves.

He had realized something.

Her clothes obscured her true figure.

"What do you think?" Nene pressed.

"If you really want to know… Um, I think it's cute."

"Right? Jhin, what about you? You could compliment me once in a blue moon."

The sniper gave Nene a passing glance.

"What?"

"Looks fine."

"Oh?!"

Iska applauded. Even Nene herself immediately yelped.

That was high praise from Jhin. He wasn't one to praise people. But Nene was that cute in a swimsuit.

CHAPTER 2

"Hee-hee. Complimented by the boys!"

"No fair, Nene!"

Captain Mismis had come around to them. She stood right in front of their eyes with her chest puffed out. She was practically asking to be looked at.

"All right, Iska, Jhin, do you like my swimsuit? Isn't it cute?"

"...Uh, yeah, but..."

Was it a kid's suit?

It sported the silhouette of a cat. It was designed with optimal cuteness.

It was more childish than Nene's swimsuit, but Mismis had a baby face and petite stature. The swimsuit suited her perfectly.

Except there was one issue.

"It *is* cute, but...but the size..."

"What size?"

"I don't think it's hiding everything, which could be a problem."

He was talking about the twin peaks jutting out of Mismis's chest. They were disproportionate to her petite form, which couldn't be hidden by a child-size swimsuit.

"Captain, something's slipping out. Right there."

"*Whaaat?* What do you think you're doing, Nene?"

With her pointer finger, Nene had poked Mismis's chest overflowing from her swimsuit. The sides and bottom of her thick curves threatened to wiggle out. Whenever Mismis took a step, they jiggled in a very...stimulating way.

"You're poisoning the children."

"Oh, I know! I know!" Nene exclaimed. "This is what you'd call 'unrepentant.'"

"An exhibitionist, you mean."

"You're all terrible!" Captain Mismis clutched her floating device in front of herself to hide her chest. "Ugh! ...Anyway! Let's get in the pool! I wanna go with the waves. We're gonna have a hundred-meter race!"

"Boss, I'm pretty sure you can't swim for that long."

"Nuh-uh! I can doggy paddle! I'm pretty good at it! I think I could break a world record."

She ditched her swim ring and ran off to the pool.

Iska, Jhin, and Nene started walking over the hot beach, following her petite stature.

They reached the briny wave pool.

"Whoa! It's super salty. It's like real ocean water!" Nene squealed, licking the spray off her lips. "Hmm. But it's not just sodium chloride. This saltiness is complex. Maybe they've made artificial ocean water with a whole list of minerals? … I should try another taste."

"Nene! Catch!"

"Whoa! W-wait, Captain!" Nene swam after the ball that Mismis had passed.

Right before the ball touched the water, Nene leaped out and skillfully kicked it with her foot.

"Hey! No feet! That's unfair, Nene."

"Hee-hee. Nobody said that was against the rules!"

Iska sent the ball back with both hands, and Jhin hit it above Mismis's head.

"Oops, I hit it too far."

"S-seriously, Jhin. That was too strong!" Mismis exclaimed.

"But you'll lose if you don't catch it, boss. Looks like dinner is on you."

"Did you do that on purpose?! …I'm not going to lose to your mean tricks!" She pushed through the water in desperation.

The pool was deep enough to touch a man's chest. Everything below Mismis's neck was below water.

CHAPTER 2

But she'd lose if the ball hit the water.

Mismis closed in on the ball at the last moment, turning to Jhin and smiling triumphantly.

"Ha-ha! Better luck next time, Jhin! I got it just in the nick of time! As payback, I'm gonna—"

"Boss. Behind you. A tidal wave."

"Excuse me? Uh! Aaaaaaaah?!"

Jhin's warning was too late. The artificial wave crashed over Mismis, swallowing her. Meaning she had no time to throw back the ball.

"We did it! You lose, Captain. I'm looking forward to dinner." Nene raised both her hands to cheer.

"Nene, watch out."

"What? Gah! So salty!" Her signature ponytail was soaking wet.

As she stood up, Nene was dripping water.

"Ugh. My hair's ruined…and my swimsuit is slipping. These strings are so tough to tie." Nene attempted to adjust her bathing suit.

…But before she could…it slipped right off her chest.

"Um…"

It splashed into the water.

Nene stared at it, and her face became cherry red.

"*Aaaaaah!* Iska, Jhin, don't look! Don't you dare!"

"Nene, that wasn't very sly," Mismis noted.

"H-hey! And you're the one to talk, Captain!" Nene clasped her chest with one hand, using the other to fish out her swimsuit. "Captain, could you help with the string…?"

"Okay. But let's get out of the pool first."

They could no longer avoid the stares of men gathering around Nene.

They headed to the beach. Under the shade of a palm tree, Mismis tied Nene's swimsuit.

"I'll go buy some drinks or something." Jhin pointed at a hidden-away beach shop. "I think coconut juice was their specialty. You good with that?"

"I'd like one," Nene said.

"Me too. What about you, Captain?" Iska asked.

"Um, I'll have the same thing... Wait. This *is* a vacation. I'm going to have something more mature—a coconut beer! That's one of their specialties, too, isn't it?"

"A beer?" Jhin's eyebrows knit dubiously. "Better not, boss. It's not for children. You'll probably collapse after a single sip."

"I'm not a kid! I'm an adult!"

"Jeez. I'm underage. Could you come with me to buy your drink, boss?"

"You can count on me! Wait under the shade, Iska, Nene." Captain Mismis started to jauntily walk across the beach with Jhin.

They watched her leave, thinking she looked exactly like a kid.

"Hey, Iska, have you ever seen the captain drink?"

"No. I think she's on island time."

She was challenging herself to do things out of her comfort zone. The atmosphere of the resort was so congenial, it brought everyone's guard down.

"I'm kind of worried she'll get too excited and take off the bandage on her shoulder, I guess. Her astral crest would definitely shock normal people, wouldn't it?" Nene asked.

"Maybe..."

There were citizens in neutral cities and independent countries who feared witches, even though their countries were diplomatic with Nebulis. The witches of Nebulis were known to conceal their crests when they were abroad.

...People with astral power have the potential to be way stronger than anyone with a gun.

...Goes to figure normal people would be scared.

There was a reason why the independent state of Alsamira allowed people to carry arms. These self-defense measures were instated to prevent the public from being afraid of immigrated witches. Because of that, Iska was able to openly bring in his astral swords.

"How's your artificial crest, Nene?"

"You almost can't see it anymore. I don't have anything covering it, but you can't tell, right?" Nene held out the back of her right hand.

It was just visible enough that Iska needed to stare closely to see it.

"And Jhin said his is gone. Looks like it depends on the person," said Nene.

"Then all we need to worry about is Captain Mismis's. And we should figure out a way to deal with it in the next sixty days..."

They *could* hide the mark from prying eyes with a bandage. But the big issue was the astral energy that seeped out. Because they couldn't hide it in their present situation, she would be caught by detectors in the Empire.

They had a sixty-day deadline.

If they didn't find a way to hide the astral power, Mismis would not be able to live in the Empire anymore. That would spell the end for Unit 907.

"We shouldn't talk to the captain about it for now. We'll do the work."

"I agree. It's been a while since I've seen her at ease." Nene leaned against the palm tree and smiled guilelessly. "And I get to hang out with you and Jhin."

"Yeah. It's been a long time since I've felt like I'm on vacation."

Because thinking back to his "breaks" in the neutral city meant Alice would be on his mind.

Even when he tried to remember the museum or the opera, all that occupied his mind was her profile—her striking features and confident smile. But most of all, he thought of her lips, which were the color of cherry blossoms, and—

...*What am I thinking?*

...*I'm at a resort to forget about my duties and obligations concerning the Sovereignty!*

Right then, Jhin came back carrying juice for everyone.

"Welcome back, Jhin. Huh? Where's Captain Mismis?"

The captain was nowhere to be seen after she'd gone with Jhin to buy beer.

"Was her order after yours or something?"

"She got caught," replied the young man with silver hair, clean and simple. "She got rounded up by the guards for questioning. They told her to get out her ID."

"Wh-what does that mean?!" Nene hounded Jhin. "Did they discover the astral crest on the captain and...? Th-that would be a disaster..."

"No, it was the beer."

"Come again?"

"She was caught for underage drinking. No one would think the boss is an adult."

"...Oh, got it," Iska replied.

"...I see," Nene said.

"Like I said, beer isn't for children," grumbled the sniper, sipping on coconut juice.

CHAPTER 2

3

The sun was setting.

As Iska headed to the hotel through the shopping areas, his cheeks were brushed by the gentle breeze.

"Iska, the wind has gotten chillier," Nene said.

"Deserts get cold in the evenings. I think it'll be colder when it's night."

Easy to heat up and to cool down, the desert sands burned like a frying pan in the afternoon and would cool like ice in the night. Meanwhile, the shopping area showed no signs of dying down, crowded by more people in the evening. The restaurants and bars were starting to really make money for the night.

"That restaurant has a long line!"

"That's what happens when it's dinnertime. Looks like it's popular. How about we go tomorrow, since Captain Mismis is tuckered out today?"

Iska walked next to Nene, holding the bag containing Mismis's swimsuit and other personal effects. As for the captain herself...

"Jhin? How's Captain Mismis?"

"She's asleep."

Captain Mismis had had the time of her life. Jhin was carrying her on his back as she snored in a cute way.

"I think the beer did it. One sip, and she was asleep."

"Nothing short of what I would expect. Oh right, Jhin, could you take the captain back to the room? We'll go buy dinner from the market over there."

"Don't get lost." Jhin walked away, shouldering the petite captain on his back.

When he passed the intersection, Nene turned right around. "Iska, c-could you wait here?! I'll be right back!"

"What? Weren't we headed to the market?"

"..." Nene wordlessly pointed to the public toilets at the intersection. "...Uh...since I had that juice earlier..."

"Take your time."

"Be right back!" Nene sprinted as fast as she could to the bathroom.

Iska stood in front of the intersection, waiting for her.

He started to remember how Captain Mismis had said she wanted to eat barbecue tomorrow. Iska vaguely noticed the light turning and—

"Ugh! There are just too many identical hotels at this resort! The maps are hard to read, and we've lost Shuvalts!"

Iska heard a girl's voice that rang like a bell. Footsteps approached from behind him.

"Ah?!"

Someone crashed into Iska from behind.

The small girl dropped her map and fell onto the road, hitting her hip.

"Oh! Are you all right?"

"Ouch... M-my apologies. I was lost and looking at the map, so..."

The girl took Iska's hand as he lifted her to her feet.

She brushed bits of sand off her elegant dress before tilting her head up in a provocative way. He took one look at her eyes.

—*Alice?*

His eyes fooled him for a moment. Iska wasn't entirely at fault.

After all, she had sweet eyes and glossy hair that was strawberry blond. Her flushed cheeks and lips were full of life. She looked like a doll.

CHAPTER 2

She must have been around fourteen or fifteen. Though she was young, she possessed a certain beauty and magnetism that reminded Iska of the Ice Calamity Witch.

"...Um?"

"...*You* are...?"

Iska had lost his ability to speak. The girl had opened her eyes wide in astonishment. There was a reason for this...

"Shhh, keep quiet. I'm gonna let you out right now."

"Why? ...Why are you...letting me escape...?"

One year prior, during a certain incident, Iska had lost his title as a Saint Disciple by letting a young witch out of prison.

And *that very girl* was in front of his eyes.

"You're from..."

"Ngh." Her shoulders quivered.

Her reaction left no room for doubt. She had clearly remembered him.

...I thought I'd never see this person again...especially here and now!

With the nature of an independent state, there was technically a chance that they would meet again. The Empire and the Sovereignty had a long past of negotiating with the country to side with them.

But he never would have expected a run-in with this young witch right after his reunion with Alice.

"..."

"..."

They both looked straight at each other, unable to utter another word. The silence signified their inner tension and turmoil.

"Sorry for the wait, Iska!"

"Whoa?!" He pivoted toward Nene, whose ponytail swayed as she dashed over.

"Huh? What's wrong?"

"W-well, um… I—I don't know her. Um… Right! She was asking me for directions."

"Who?"

"What? That…"

He finally realized that the girl had already left his side, running across the street as if to escape.

Her brilliant blond hair almost immediately disappeared into the crowd.

"…"

"Iska, what's wrong?"

"…Uh, nothing. We need to go shop at the market. Move it, Nene."

He nudged Nene from behind as she tilted her head quizzically, getting her to start walking.

The roads were growing hot. He thought about where the witch had gone, weaving through the streets by herself…

CHAPTER 3

A Prayer to the Planet by Sisbell the Witch

1

As one of the three daughters born under Mirabella, who was the eighth queen of the Nebulis Sovereignty, Sisbell Lou Nebulis IX was blessed with powers as a direct descendant of the Founder.

She had Illumination.

She could play back events that occurred within the past twenty years within a thousand-foot radius. Her astral power was one of the time-space interference variety and was especially rare among that type of power.

"*...Do you know of the rumors about the queen?*"

"*I heard she wants to pass down the throne to Princess Aliceliese—not to the eldest princess or to the youngest one.*"

She didn't let even a trivial piece of conversation slide in the royal palace.

Weaponizing her ability to snoop out information, she had once caught a spy from the Empire.

"Princess Sisbell, you have been commanded to go on an expedition to the independent state of Alsamira."

She was in the palace—the "Queen's Space."

Sunlight streamed onto the houseplants and flowers that decorated the sacred space. A voice echoed through the area.

The current queen, Mirabella.

The queen was her biological mother, but they were not allowed to speak on familial terms.

"We've received information that the desert country is proactively accepting people from the Empire."

"Yes."

"Alsamira is not like the neutral cities. They have not declared neutrality… Under certain conditions, they may choose to become an Imperial state."

That would make them an enemy of the Sovereignty.

Because of that, Sisbell had been chosen for dispatch.

With the astral power of Illumination, Sisbell could even reproduce verbatim secret meetings that occurred in the state.

In other words, they would be able to eavesdrop on their meetings.

"It's your duty to determine if they are sleeping with the enemy. Out of concern for your safety during this expedition, I will send one of my guards with you."

"Please do not worry about me." Sisbell politely turned down the queen's offer.

She didn't need a guard.

To be more exact, Sisbell did not trust her subordinates in the Sovereignty.

"I will do just fine with my keeper, Shuvalts. I will be acting the part of a tourist. There will be no reason for them to suspect me if I can help it."

"Understood." The queen let a sigh leave her lips.

She had thought as much. Her sigh must have expelled a combination of worry and exasperation. It was difficult for Sisbell to watch her mother's face when she was like that.

...I'm sorry, Mother... I have reasons that I can't tell even you.

She was doing this to *protect her mother's life*.

Sisbell couldn't allow anyone into her heart within the Sovereignty—even her oldest sister, Elletear, or Aliceliese.

"Then I will take my absence from the castle."

"I will leave the matter to you."

Sisbell turned her back on the queen. *Please stay safe while I am away*, she wished from the very bottom of her heart.

But Sisbell couldn't say it out loud, so she swallowed her words in silence.

2

It all started with simple curiosity.

With the astral power of Illumination, Sisbell Lou Nebulis IX could re-create anything that had occurred within a thousand-foot radius and a twenty-year span.

Every secret deal in the royal palace could be seen by her.

Which meant the public only had the option to hold these meetings away from the royal palace, putting them beyond range.

Sisbell had been waiting for them to walk right into her net, caught up in the lies that she'd spread herself.

...Don't underestimate me... I'll show you the true power of the Revered Founder and her descendants.

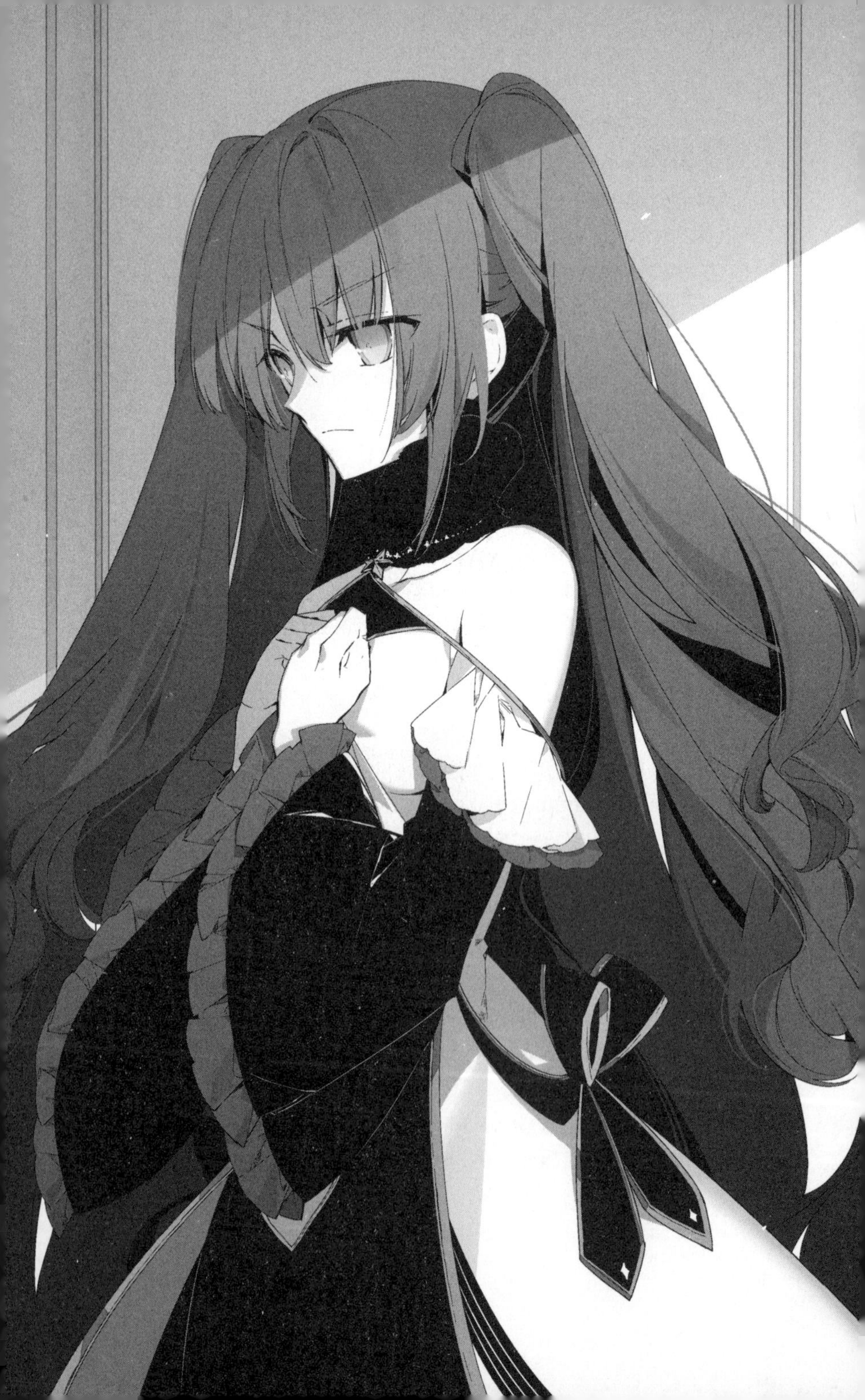

CHAPTER 3

Because Sisbell could reproduce the events occurring within a *thousand feet and twenty years* of her location.

Even if the noble families were conversing outside the royal castle to avoid her prying eyes, Sisbell knew all about them.

All because she was curious about trivial conversations.

Sisbell, who was sociable and overflowing with intellectual curiosity, had just wanted to know what kinds of conversations others were having.

It had broken her.

She had been burdened with information from a power on par with omniscience. This knowledge included dark schemes and the existence of unspeakable "monsters" beyond her imagination. It was too much for an innocent girl of fifteen to shoulder.

It was *no longer human*.

There was a monster hidden within the royal family of the Nebulis Sovereignty. Though it wore the mask of a human, when the time came, it would fling off its disguise and reveal its true nature.

And steal the country from the queen herself.

…Her life is in danger… But if I tell her, they would only begin by targeting me.

The Nebulis Sovereignty would collapse.

Not from the Imperial Army. But from those who targeted the queen's life. The three bloodlines—the Lou, Zoa, and Hydra Houses—would have nothing to do with it.

The royal family itself could be destroyed by that monster.

"…Stay brave, Sisbell. I will protect my mother. Who else would be able to protect her?"

She was in a corner of her room.

Sisbell was shivering on that day and chanting as though trying to convince herself. It couldn't be her oldest sisters, Elletear or Aliceliese. She had no idea who was the mastermind behind this plan.

Though Sisbell knew one of the people who was part of the scheme, she didn't know how many more in the Sovereignty were traitors.

...If my sister Alice is a traitor, that would be the most dangerous situation... If she wanted to, even our mother would be...

Aliceliese's power had surpassed the current queen's skills.

If she planned to overthrow the government and the queen, she could easily succeed at a coup d'état. That was why Sisbell had turned into a recluse. She couldn't leave the country. Even during the times when her sister Elletear was traveling abroad or Aliceliese was heading to the battlefield, Sisbell elected to not leave the royal palace.

She was entirely engrossed with the idea of protecting her mother.

"If I'm by my mother's side, the traitors shouldn't lay a hand on her..."

She would protect her mother—and the country.

That was the resolve that Sisbell could tell no one about.

"...But..."

She continued to search alone for the traitors planning to overthrow the country, locked away in her room. She was under pressure, never knowing when her life might be in jeopardy.

It was too harsh for a fifteen-year-old girl to handle.

"Isn't there anyone who's on my side...?" She held a handkerchief to her mouth to conceal her sobs.

Someone. Anyone! Wasn't there a knight in this world to support her...?

Though her astral power was expansive, it served little in battle. Her only confidant was her keeper, who was too old to possibly fight.

Sisbell's physical strength was as good as nonexistent.

"Where can I find…a strong ally…?"

She needed powerful subordinates in the Sovereignty to challenge the monster and the traitors who followed it. But the people in the royal palace wouldn't suffice. She hadn't been able to identify the traitors, which meant she couldn't heedlessly ask them for help.

"…" She hugged her own knees, which she couldn't stop from trembling. "…Who can I rely on…?"

She had no allies. At least, not in this country.

Because of that, she recalled something that had happened a year ago.

She ended up thinking about the Imperial soldier who had let her out of prison.

"I've got a thing or two to say about the Empire's policy of rounding up all the astral mages, especially someone like you. You're still a kid."

The Saint Disciple Iska.

Though he was under the direct command of the throne, he had helped a captured witch.

…Back then, I was hiding my astral powers… Did he just think I was weak?

Why had he let her escape?

The reason was still unclear, but she thought it over suddenly. Though she knew it was just a convenient fantasy and an easy escape, she couldn't help but let her imagination expand.

If he was here… If the man who saved her was here, could he become her ally?

3

Back to the present.

In the urban area of Alsamira, Princess Sisbell forgot to breathe as she looked up at the boy in front of her.

"..."

She gazed at his dark-brown hair and gentle face that didn't look like it belonged to an Imperial soldier. His face was unmistakable. He was the Saint Disciple Iska—the one she had happened on a year ago.

This wasn't Imperial territory. Because he was wearing his own clothing instead of his battle uniform, she had thought it was just someone who looked like him.

"You're from..."

"Ngh." Sisbell's eyes opened wide as he mumbled.

I knew it! He's that Saint Disciple!

If they had been out of the public eye, she would have shouted that at the top of her lungs. She didn't care what kind of fate had brought him here.

He was her only beacon of hope.

Maybe.

This swordsman was the *only* one she could rely on. He was the only person she knew outside of the Sovereignty.

Fight fire with fire.

To stand against the monster in the Sovereignty, it would be necessary to bring in a blazing fire from outside the country—especially someone who was the strongest, highest-ranking soldier in battle, especially a Saint Disciple.

"Uh, um...!" she rasped, too nervous to speak out.

CHAPTER 3

She tried desperately to force her voice to come out of her dry mouth.

"Sorry for the wait, Iska!"

An unfamiliar girl sporting a ponytail had run up to them.

Was she one of the swordsman's acquaintances? That would mean she was also an Imperial soldier.

This was bad.

"Nh." She gritted her molars and turned her back to him to run down the intersection.

Anyone from the Empire was an enemy. That still hadn't changed. Sisbell wanted to talk to Iska, and she didn't plan on trusting anyone else from the Imperial military.

...I have no reason to panic.

...The Saint Disciple Iska is here. That by itself was incredibly worthwhile to learn.

"My lady!"

After Sisbell crossed the street, her black-suited attendant called out to her. He was her keeper, Shuvalts. With his neat salt-and-pepper hair, the elderly man ran over to her, out of breath.

"I was searching for you. I beg you: Do not push my old body."

"...I found him."

"Pardon?"

"Listen, Shuvalts! I've finally found him—my dream guard!" Sisbell sprinted over to the old man in the suit as though to hug him in her arms.

As Rin was with Aliceliese, this old gentleman had accompanied Sisbell since her youth. He was her one and only subordinate in the Sovereignty who she trusted with all her heart.

"Oh, I have no idea where to start…" She couldn't slow down.

Her wildest dreams had actually manifested. Now that she had gotten this far, she would make sure to see this through.

"Shuvalts, there's something I must discuss with you immediately. Let's get back to the hotel first."

She grabbed the older gentleman by the hand and started striding toward the shopping area.

"We'll wait until nightfall... I'll make sure we succeed. For the sake of our country."

She would be the next queen.

Sisbell Lou Nebulis IX would protect both the current queen and the country.

4

The frosty wind whistled in the great desert of the east.

The sunset burned on the horizon, and the curtain of night drew closed over the sky.

Though the shopping areas of Alsamira were still illuminated by glaring neon lights, there were not as many people as there had been in the afternoon. Most of the tourists had gone back to their hotels to go to sleep.

"*Achoo!*"

"My lady. I recall I informed you the desert cools at night."

"Yes, I underestimated how cold it would get..." She nodded in agreement with the older man who walked beside her.

Though she regretted her choice of a thin dress, Sisbell did not allow her pace to slow as she stalked down the streets.

...I'm always holed up in the warm royal palace.

...I wonder how long it's been since I've walked outside at night.

CHAPTER 3

There was a part of her that feared for their safety.

Since Shuvalts was an astral mage, he could handle a small scuffle. But if they happened across a group of thieves carrying guns, they would be in a bit of trouble.

...This is when I wish I had stronger astral power... Not that I'm complaining about mine.

The mages were born with their powers.

Even among the descendants of the Founder, there was a large difference between these natural-born powers, particularly their use in battle.

For generations, the queen of Nebulis wished for powers that were suitable in battle, because they could lead the astral corps against an Imperial Army invasion.

"I'll totally turn these customs on their head..." She balled her hands into fists in the cold.

Sisbell continued to walk down the illuminated road and eventually arrived at the familiar intersection—where she had come upon the Saint Disciple Iska earlier that day.

"Fortunately, no one else is around. It's too cold. They're all in taverns."

"We can't be careless. Make sure to stand guard, Shuvalts."

She couldn't let anyone see this.

Even outside the Imperial territories, some citizens feared witches. Basically, there was no advantage to anyone finding out about her powers.

"Please show me your past, planet."

Beneath Sisbell's collarbone and near her chest, her astral power started to glow through her thin dress and into the empty night.

The light gathered. Like a projector, the image of a lone boy formed in the air.

*　*　*

"Iska, what's wrong?"

"...Uh, nothing. We need to go shop at the market. Move it, Nene."

The boy with dark-brown hair nudged the back of the girl with the ponytail and started to leave. Sisbell could even reproduce their images walking, which meant she could track their movements. That was another part of her powers.

"Is this him?"

"Yes, let's go, Shuvalts."

They followed after Iska. Even if someone else witnessed this, it would seem as though Iska was actually on that road.

...The girl called Nene must be an Imperial soldier... But I don't think Iska has told her about me.

Iska and Nene strolled through the shopping area.

They had an easygoing conversation as they headed to a market. After buying things that seemed to be their dinner, they were back on the street again.

Sisbell had thought Iska would mention her in that time.

"He hasn't even said I'm a witch. I guess he was working alone a year ago."

Iska had lost his position as a Saint Disciple due to the incident where he broke her out.

Which also meant he had been the only one who'd been punished.

Even to this Nene girl, he couldn't just talk about that event. After all, she might be suspected as a coconspirator if she knew the details.

"They're staying at the Germrick Hotel," her keeper noted.

Iska brought them right to the hotel.

Looking up at the building that towered over him, Shuvalts quietly started to murmur. "A well-established hotel corporation.

CHAPTER 3

They own hotels in resorts all over the world. Their ratings are often average or higher."

"Which makes it an appropriate choice for an Imperial soldier on vacation?"

"If he was here on secret orders, Imperial headquarters would have put him up in a higher-rated hotel. Or they would have chosen an Imperial hotel."

But that wasn't the case.

Iska hadn't come to Alsamira as a part of his duties.

"That makes things easier. We'll go through with the plan, Shuvalts."

"Are you sure you will do this alone?"

"Yes. I want to discuss this with him alone. If both of us go, it'll just put him on guard."

...I can't believe I'm sneaking into a boy's room in the middle of the night... My face is burning. I'm so embarrassed.

Sisbell grounded herself and headed to the hotel lobby.

Using her astral power, she found out the room number that he had headed toward. She made sure he had gone inside alone.

He was on the fourth floor.

With stifled footsteps, she inched down the silent hallway.

"This is it..." She held the key card over the door's sensor.

Sisbell had pretended to be Iska's girlfriend and gotten her hands on the key in exchange for a large wad of money.

It opened.

She held her breath as she put her hand on the door and slowly pushed it open.

The corridor was dim. Beyond it, she could see the living room was unlit. He must be already asleep.

...It's better that way... I would prefer it over him noticing the door opening.

With her hands, she felt her way down the hallway.

Once her eyes had adjusted to the darkness, Sisbell approached the bed in the back of the room.

"Um...excuse me..."

Would he be surprised if she called him by name? What could she say to him while he was asleep? She reached out to the bed, unable to figure out what to say.

"An assassin, huh?"

What?

Why had his voice come from behind?

She didn't even have time to think about it as she felt an impact against her shoulder. Her world started spinning, and she felt faint for a moment.

"Nh?!"

When she realized it, Sisbell was being pinned down to the carpet. He was straddling her as she was lying faceup.

"Who are you working for? The Sovereignty? Or is it—?"

"Y-you've got it wrong! This is a misunderstanding! I'm not planning on doing anything!"

Since he was on top of her, she couldn't move an inch. He closed his hands around her throat.

Sisbell desperately yelled out with her mouth, the only free part of her body.

"I just came here to see you, Saint Disciple Iska. I have something to ask of you!"

"...?"

The lights came on.

She caught sight of the boy who had pushed her down.

He was in the same clothes from the afternoon.

Though it was late at night, he still hadn't even taken a shower, much less gone to bed.

CHAPTER 3

"Wait... You're..."

"It's been a whole year."

Iska was taken aback.

When she sensed he had loosened his hold on her, Sisbell flashed him a big smile to hide her nerves.

"Saint Disciple Iska, I have something I must ask you," she repeated, pressed on the ground.

Sisbell addressed the boy who looked down at her.

"Would you accompany me to the Sovereignty?"

INTERMISSION

Three Sisters

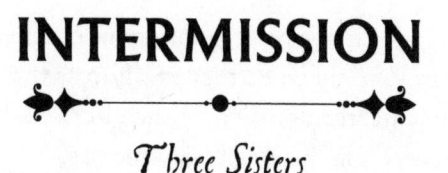

1

The Imperial capital. Yunmelngen.

This was possibly the most well-known place in the world.

It had once been burned to the ground during a rebellion led by the Founder Nebulis. But it had risen out of the ashes like a phoenix, laying the foundations for this steel city. And the name came from none other than the divine ruler of the Empire.

Sector Two. The business district.

A huge man had come to visit one of the restaurants that had established itself within the zone—called the Powder Base.

He was more of a tank than a man.

Over six and a half feet tall, he had a burly torso. His rippling muscles seemed to encase his body like armor, and he had to be more than two hundred pounds. His tattered clothes made him look like an escapee from jail, and he was covered by a hood from the neck up.

The room stirred.

He didn't seem to notice when the restaurant started to get louder. The giant accepted a plastic bag from a frightened waitress and left.

Then he headed to the park, ignoring the children, whose faces had stiffened from fright when they saw him as they played in the afternoon. He hunkered down on a bench in the back of the park.

"…" He silently ate the bread from the bag.

It was just a tiny loaf of bread.

Based on his large build, it seemed entirely too small. A normal person would think that it was near impossible for him to maintain his figure on these small portions.

However…for the Saint Disciple of the ninth seat from Heaven's Prison, this was the *limit* of consumable energy.

Statulle converted too much energy—anything he ingested would be absorbed ten times more than the average person. Had he eaten a normal person's meal, he would have been consuming *too many* calories and bulking up more.

He was blessed with anabolic steroids in his body.

He had no need to train.

If he worked out like a normal person, his flesh would disintegrate from the strain. It was the same phenomenon as a whale being crushed under its own weight on land.

He had capabilities that surpassed any form of doping. In other words, he had an unparalleled body.

"Statulle. Been a while since I've seen you sunbathing."

A bearded man in his thirties or forties had called out to the giant from behind the bench. He was the diametric opposite of the giant, thin as a withered branch. He donned a white coat like a researcher's over his delicate shoulders, which seemed fragile enough to break if so much as a breeze blew.

"How is it basking in the sun? It's been two months, right? Any thoughts?"

"...It's too bright," he boomed, loud enough for the ground to almost quake. "...And too hot."

"You've only got your body to blame. But it's not all bad. I think you're the only one who could withstand that freezing cage in just a shirt."

Heaven's Prison.

Statulle was the guard of the underground jail dedicated to detaining witches and sorcerers who had been caught by the Empire.

"You're always trouble..."

"Hmm? Me?"

"There's no way you're just out on a stroll. What do you want?"

The other man was the Saint Disciple of the tenth seat—Sir Karosos Newton, the head of the research facility. He was known as the most depraved researcher in the Department of Weapons Development in Sector Three.

"Just to have a quick chat with you."

"..."

"About a purebred. One of the daughters from the royal family of Nebulis has wandered to another country by herself."

"All alone?"

"She's only accompanied by her keeper. If she doesn't have a guard, she might as well be alone."

The head of the lab sat down on the bench.

"Which means that they've practically handed her over to us."

"..."

"The source is from the Sovereignty itself. I'd like to know myself who betrayed them, but the Eight Great Apostles dodged the question. They told me to figure it out myself, since I'm a Saint Disciple."

"...That sounds about right."

"Putting that aside, we'll need a plan to capture that witch."

The skeleton of a man sighed dramatically.

"It's not the ideal place. She's in a resort in the desert called Alsamira. We would never go there if not for this opportunity. But headquarters is reluctant to dispatch troops."

"To a colony?" asked Statulle.

"Call them allies... Well, this one is an independent state."

Colonies were autonomous entities that were nonetheless officially under Imperial control.

Allies were independent states on relatively equal footing with the Empire.

The Empire didn't recognize the former. They wanted to remove all witches from the world, which could be accomplished better through the eradication of power dynamics and hierarchies.

However...the guard of Heaven's Prison had just pointed out the Empire's true stance.

"They say sending troops would cause a fuss—*if* the unthinkable happened."

If they engaged in war at a resort, they would be the target of criticism from other countries. It would have been different if the Empire was the same superpower from a century prior. But these days, such an incident could potentially give the Sovereignty an opportunity to advance their own interests.

"Normally, Nameless would be the ideal individual for this mission, but he is currently on a covert mission in the Sovereignty. Why don't we make use of the new weapon to capture our target? You know the one. The experimental device we installed in Heaven's Prison," suggested the lab technician.

"...You mean the Witch Hunter?" asked the burly man.

"I want to borrow it. There's no evidence that thing was built by the Empire. It wouldn't be too hard to maintain plausible deniability even if there are a few eyewitness accounts. And it would be the perfect tool to capture her."

"It'll come at a high price."

"Naturally." The researcher nodded in satisfaction.

"A purebred, huh? Looking forward to seeing what kind of witch we catch."

2

A century ago, Nebulis I—the younger twin sister of the Founder—had led the astral mages in place of her exhausted sister and created the Sovereignty.

There were three families who had inherited that first generation's blood: the Lou, the Zoa, and the Hydra.

The members of these three families were what the Empire called the "purebreds," the most dangerous witches who warranted the highest level of caution.

"How pitiful… This is devastating," mumbled a man, walking through the passageway.

In all black and concealed by a mask, he turned up to the heavens dramatically.

"The Lou, the Zoa, the Hydra. We have strong bloodlines and yet, when it comes to our battles with the Empire, we are unable to join forces. Even though we are kindred who all follow in the footsteps of the Revered Founder and Revered Progenitor."

He was in the Moon Spire of the royal palace in Nebulis.

It was the domain of the House of Zoa, a mere two hundred

yards removed from the Star Spire where the current queen lived with Alice and her two sisters.

"The Star, Moon, and Solar Spires. We each seclude ourselves in our own towers and refuse to interact except during times of governance. What a wretched state... But then again..."

Lord Mask On. A member of the Zoa House. An unmistakable purebred.

He continued lightly. "Regardless of the situation, you are the only one who always comes to see us."

"Should I consider this a warm reception?"

"Of course." His smile could be taken as sarcasm or sincerity. Lord Mask nodded at the princess who had come alone to the Moon Spire. "I welcome your visit from the very depths of my heart, eldest daughter of the Lou."

"Thank you."

Her wavy hair was emerald with hints of the purest veins of gold in the world. She was easily a hand—or perhaps a fist—taller than her younger sister Alice. Her curves were more matured than Alice's, too, to the point that they were almost spilling out of her royal garb.

Her gentle smile gave off the impression of a grounded adult. If Alice was said to have evolved from a girl to a young lady, this princess was the final form of that progression.

"It has been a while, Elletear. I heard you just returned from an expedition yesterday."

"It has been too long, my lord."

Elletear Lou Nebulis IX. The oldest of the three Lou sisters.

She pulled up the hem of her dress slightly, letting it flutter as she bowed. She was twenty this year. She had a confident grace about her and beautiful features that made her one of the most likely contenders for the right to the throne in the conclave, along with her younger sister Alice.

And if I had to say it... She is the largest threat to the Zoa household as we aim to take the throne.

It wasn't just in Lord Mask's imagination that she had become more charming during the half year she'd spent away from the castle.

"I came back solely because I wanted to see you, my lord."

"That pleases me. All the youth are tempted by your beauty. Since the occasion has presented itself, we should have a long discussion in the parlor."

He wasn't just being polite. The servants walking through the halls of the House of Zoa were unintentionally stopping to ogle Elletear's sensational figure.

It wasn't just the men. Even the young women were holding their breaths at her beauty.

"This way."

"Thank you. And where is Lady Kissing? I know she's taken a liking to you. I haven't seen her in a while. I would like to greet her."

"Unfortunately, she is still shy around strangers. She is a troubled child."

Kissing Zoa Nebulis. The House of Zoa's prided secret weapon was still being fine-tuned. Meaning she was mentally unstable, far from a state that could be allowed near others. Not that they planned to divulge that detail to the Lou, even if she had already been adjusted.

The pair entered the parlor.

"Let me get you a drink. Would you like coffee or some tea?"

"Water. Please."

"Water? It seems your tastes have changed."

"I'm exhausted from my travels." Elletear smiled in embarrassment, placing a hand on her cheek. "I visited many towns and tasted their local coffees and teas. While I am at home, I would prefer to have a less stimulating beverage."

"I see. You. Please fetch some," ordered Lord Mask to the servant behind them, who nodded reverently and left the room.

He checked that the door had closed shut. "Right. I look forward to hearing of your travels."

Lord Mask sat down on the sofa across from her.

"It was longer than usual. Nearly six months. Didn't that worry the queen?"

"She's used to it. This is just one of the duties of a princess."

The descendants of the Founder were objects of admiration and often an aspirational goal for astral mages everywhere. If Elletear was to pay a visit to anyone in the Nebulis Sovereignty, even inhabitants of the most backwater regions would come out to greet her.

And it would increase support for the conclave.

It was common knowledge among the Zoa and Hydra Houses that the number of influential people supporting Elletear was growing by the day.

"I suppose the reception was excellent?"

"Yes. On this excursion, I gained a better understanding of the apprehension in the remote regions. Although the central state is safe, the other states are concerned about when the Empire might strike."

"...Yes. And there was the incident with Salinger the Transcendental."

"When I heard that it was the Imperial Army that released him, I almost doubted my ears. Everyone is concerned about how the Empire could have broken past our country's borders." Elletear shook her head in gloom.

It was *obvious*. Lord Mask had been asking if her campaigning for the conclave was going well.

She hadn't failed to notice his implication.

That's not why I've been going on these trips! Aliceliese would have vehemently denied it if she'd been in Elletear's place.

But the eldest sister was unfazed, redirecting the conversation with ease.

"..."

"What is it, my lord? You're smiling."

"Nothing. I was simply thinking of how Alice might have replied in your place."

"My, Lord Mask. Are you that interested in her?" Elletear smiled in a suggestive way that rivaled Lord Mask's. "That's perfect. Weren't you the one speaking about this earlier? Why can't the three families of descendants join forces against the Empire?"

"Yes, exactly."

If the three families could unite to attack the Empire, the capital might become a sea of flames again.

But it would result in a great number of casualties.

The ones who wanted to avoid these deaths were the House of Lou, the ones who currently were led by the queen. They put up defensive measures against Imperial attacks in their own country, attempting to limit the number of sacrifices from their astral corps.

On the other hand, the Zoa were extremists. They believed there was no greater pursuit than annihilating the Empire in battle, no matter the cost.

The House of Hydra were moderates. Though they were involved in the fight for the throne between the other two Houses, they would follow any recognized queen when it came down to it.

"I agree. Aside from the conclave."

"Hmm?"

Elletear had anticipated this as she brushed aside her golden waves of hair.

"I have an earnest request for you, my lord."

If she didn't have a clear reason, why would the House of Lou come all the way to visit the Zoa?

"Will you hear me out?"

"Of course. Since you came all the way to visit, I will happily lend you what strength I can."

"Well, I am pleased." The princess with emerald hair leaned forward in her seat.

It was as though she was showing her full chest to tempt him. But the masked man did not so much as flinch at that.

"To get right to the point, there are those in our country with ties to the Empire. I imagine you are aware of that."

"I have considered that possibility. But trying to expose them now is—"

"They are *my sisters*," Elletear practically sang and broke into a noble smile.

"...What did you just say?" replied Lord Mask in a strained voice.

He must have been shocked.

"Elletear..."

"I'll say it again. The ones in contact with the Empire are my sisters, Alice and Sisbell."

She planted her hands on the table and stared at the masked man.

"Just contact for now. They aren't Imperial pawns. But I am convinced they will betray us soon."

"...You sure about that?"

"I swear on my right to the throne."

"..."

Out of all the *candidates* who Lord Mask had narrowed down, those two princesses hadn't made the list.

"But how do you know? You must not have had access to this information while you were far from the palace."

"Oh, I can't tell you that. It's a secret," she said, placing a hand against her beautiful face and answering innocently to ease the tension. "It's something I've spent years building up. I can't reveal my tricks."

"...I see. Apologies." He smirked under the mask.

She would be a bad princess if she was willing to confidently inform him of her tricks. Obviously. She was the eldest sister of the House of Lou, a direct competition for the Zoa. Otherwise, she wouldn't be in the ring for the conclave.

"And what can I do?" he asked.

"To be frank, I am devastated by this news. I couldn't believe those two would be attempting to betray our mother." Her lips parted for a gentle sigh. She closed her eyes and turned her face down. "I cannot believe my beloved sisters would become barbarians... It is my duty as their sister to correct their ways. However, I am sympathetic to them."

"..."

"When the time comes, I will not be able to make the proper decision. I would like to ask you to do it, my lord."

"I see. I understand." He nodded with dramatic flair. "You need someone to send them off in your place."

"...I fear that is the case." Elletear continued to stare at the ground.

Was it to hide her devastation? Or had her lips taken on a devilish smile?

To cooperate across two Houses meant...Lord Mask and Elletear would be coconspirators.

When it would be time for the conclave, the other two princesses would be in Elletear's way. And this posed as the perfect opportunity for Lord Mask to eliminate two players from the race. This arrangement was mutually beneficial.

"Elletear, it must have been so difficult to keep this to yourself." He took her hand and gave it a gentle squeeze. "Lift your face. Leave the rest to me."

"...Which means?"

"I will keep this news in mind. I have heard Sisbell is currently out of the country. I will go after the girl myself and determine the truth."

"I am grateful for you." She revealed her puffy eyes.

Was she pretending to cry? Or had she really been concerned about the fate of her sisters?

Though he was unable to determine the truth, it did not affect the actions of the House of Zoa.

"I will help you hurt the Empire. In order to do that, we must draw out all who have ties to them."

"Yes. And I leave my sisters in your care."

At the same time. The Star Spire of Nebulis. The tower of residence for the current representatives of the queen in the House of Lou.

Alice's breathing was feeble as she lay collapsed on a sofa.

"I've depleted all energy..."

She was pale. She almost didn't want to bother breathing. Not even a single finger could move.

"...*Sniff.* I'm having the worst day ever."

She had even been moved to tears.

From morning to night, she had been trying to accomplish her duties as a princess. None of it was enjoyable or worthwhile. Why was she being tortured?

"Maybe I'll quit being a princess..."

INTERMISSION

"You have a meeting with the queen starting at five in the morning tomorrow. Noble families and guests of honor from various countries will be in attendance. About twenty in total. Please remember to think of greetings for each of them."

"Rin! Do you have a heart of stone?"

"What are you going on about? I'm rubbing your shoulders and back in appreciation of your efforts."

Alice was lying facedown. Rin was on top of her, thoroughly massaging her shoulders and back.

"Ugh... I don't understand why a seventeen-year-old princess has to suffer from stiff shoulders..."

"It comes with the job." The attendant continued to massage Alice. "Please take a bath after this and rest for the evening."

"...Okay."

"Because you *are* waking up tomorrow at four."

"You didn't have to say that *now*!" Alice screeched, placing her hands over both her ears as though she refused to listen.

You know what? I'm taking a break tomorrow! Rin can't wake me up if I freeze every last window and door that leads into my room...!

Ding, gently rang a calling bell.

Who would be calling so late at night? Alice jumped from the sofa at the voice that came from beyond the door.

"Alice."

"*M-Mother?!* Rin! H-hurry and get the door!"

"A-at once!" Rin rushed over to open the door.

It was Mirabella Lou Nebulis IIX. In a light-purple outfit, Alice's biological mother was standing in front of her room without even a guard.

"My queen! Wh-what brings you here at this time of night?!" Alice stammered.

"Some business. Alice, come with me." The queen beckoned her over, asking Alice to come out of the room.

"What happened, Mother?"

"I have two topics to discuss with you," she almost whispered. "One concerns a report, and the other is something I would like to consult you about. Which would you like to hear first?"

"—" Alice stealthily traded a look with Rin.

She had a bad feeling about this. This was a trick that her mother often used to mentally prepare the person for a conversation.

...This can't be good news... Especially if it was important enough to bring her to my room in the middle of the night.

"Whichever is easier for you to talk about."

"Then we'll start with the report. It is about the sorcerer you captured at Alcatroz."

"...Hmm?"

Salinger the Transcendental. A dangerous man who had astral power that could steal others' powers. Thirty years earlier, young Queen Mirabella had captured him, but a certain event had let him break out of prison.

It had occurred only ten days ago.

"You prevented that man's escape from the prison spire. That was an important accomplishment... Rin, I thank you for risking your life."

"N-not at all!" Rin said, straightening her posture. Her voice wasn't very strong. That was because Rin had been the one who had been saved.

"Just this once...

"...I'll lend you a hand. This guy is Alice's enemy, right?"

INTERMISSION

* * *

If Iska had not been there, they wouldn't have succeeded in stopping the sorcerer. Alice's mother would have never dreamed that an Imperial soldier had been involved in this achievement.

"What about that incident, Mother?"

To Alice, the whole thing was already over.

Salinger had fallen from the prison spire, had been arrested by the jail guards, and taken to another edifice the same day. He had been jailed once again.

"The cell is *empty*," said the queen.

"What does that mean?"

"We just received communications from the prison spire that had been housing him. The prison guards had apparently brought in an elaborate puppet made from astral power."

"I-is this really true?!" Rin was unable to keep herself from interjecting. "Iska and I... I mean, *Lady Alice* and I worked so desperately to capture him! Were the prison guards tricked and let him get away?!"

"As the sorcerer does. You cannot blame the prison guards." The queen sighed.

They could hardly imagine the dignified queen doing that, even though they were looking directly at her.

"We are currently in the process of hunting him down. Please make sure to keep this in mind—both of you. That man may appear in the palace."

"I will remember that."

If Alice were in his position, she didn't think she would target the palace.

...*I don't think he expected to get hurt by Iska... Because his defeat set him back from the starting line.*

Salinger had to be more cautious than ever.

Even if he came to the palace, he would wait for the perfect opportunity.

"Mother, is the other topic related to Salinger?"

"No, an entirely separate matter. Family business. I would like you to come with me. Rin... You should accompany us." Her eyes swept over to the end of the hall.

Nebulis IIX walked briskly down the hall. Alice nodded at Rin and followed after her.

"Mother, where are we going?"

"Haven't you seen this?" The queen turned and spread her hand to show an intricate and delicate crystal key in her palm.

Though it looked very similar to Alice's own room key, hers was made from a different gem.

"For Lady Sisbell's room," Rin offered. "But Lady Sisbell should have left the country yesterday morning."

"Which is why it is in my possession."

The queen kept going down the hallway, heading for Sisbell's room, the Small Looking Glass.

They stood in front of her door.

"Alice, what do you think of Sisbell lately?"

"What?" Alice balked when her mother suddenly asked.

Sisbell locked herself in her room, refusing to come out. Even when they occasionally ran into each other in the hallway, she would turn tail and scamper away immediately.

...If I was to be honest, Sisbell has been acting strange...and dodgy...and unfriendly...

Alice was aware how odd it was to think this about her own sister. And it wasn't her style to talk ill of people behind their backs.

"Don't you think she's been acting suspiciously?" her mother offered.

"...!" Alice doubted her own ears.

Standing next to them, Rin gaped at the queen's face in surprise.

"I am the queen. I want you and Sisbell to maintain a certain degree of dignity as part of the royal family. But I am also your mother," she said, looking almost embarrassed.

She was a mother and a queen—a woman who was torn between both roles.

"Right now, the retainers do not trust Sisbell much. I imagine she will have a difficult time during the conclave. We cannot do much about that, but as her mother, I have the duty to raise her well."

"...So you're going into her room?"

"Yes, I want to check on her activities in isolation."

Mirabella was doing this as her mother. And she had dragged Alice along to fulfill the duty of sisterhood.

"What about Lady Elletear?"

"She wasn't in her room. I don't want too many people to snoop in Sisbell's room. We'll just do it alone, since it's not an investigation."

She stuck the crystal key into the lock.

It was one that couldn't be duplicated. The key had been made by an expert craftsman, the one and only key that could open this exact door.

It unlocked.

The queen herself pushed past it and turned on the light.

...I hate that we're prying... But I have to follow my mother's wishes.

Alice sauntered into the living room after the queen. It was decorated in the style of a suite in a luxury hotel, which wasn't too different from Alice's room. If there was one dissimilarity, it was the stuffed animals tucked in corners and lining the sofas.

Sisbell would be sixteen this year. Aliceliese was only two years older than her sister, but she still felt that it seemed too juvenile to collect dolls at fifteen, especially for a princess.

"It is very clean...," Rin modestly offered to the queen, scanning the area. "I don't see much that looks out of the ordinary."

"She must have expected me to come in here and cleaned up anything that would have aroused suspicion... What *is* she doing all the time in her room? I wish there was a clue." The queen sighed again before walking over to the bathroom and washrooms. "Let's split up. Alice, Rin, you examine her bedroom."

"Yes, Mother."

She couldn't get on board with the idea of poking around her sister's bedroom, but upon investigation, the interior turned out to be immaculate. Her sheets were impressively wrinkle-free. The only things at her bedside were a pitcher and a cup.

"It's cleaner than your bed, Lady Alice."

"Rin, this isn't the time or the place for that. And my bed is clean."

If anything, this was too sterile.

Alice had a habit of reading before going to bed, bringing her favorite books with her and nodding off while reading.

"That's right. If it were me, I would stick it under my pillow so my mother wouldn't... What?"

Dink. As Alice ran her fingers under the pillow, she had touched something.

Was it a book? It felt more like a thin magazine.

She pulled it right out, then felt all the blood draining from her face.

The periodical reported on an event from a year ago.

"Iska, the Youngest Saint Disciple in History."

"Imprisoned for treason against the nation and aiding the escape of a witch. Given a life sentence."

It was familiar. It wasn't a story suited to this frank description. "Why is this...?"

Alice had obtained the same periodical when she ordered Rin to investigate the identity of an Imperial soldier named Iska.

...That's strange! Why would Sisbell have the same magazine?! ...And why would it be important enough for her to hide it under her pillow?

Next to her, Rin's face tensed.

There was no mistaking it—this periodical implied that Sisbell had been looking into the former Saint Disciple.

But why?

"No way... Did she see us together in the neutral city? It's possible with her astral powers!"

Princess Aliceliese had a connection with Iska.

Of course, their encounters had all happened by chance, but even these meetings were more than enough to tarnish her reputation. Worst case, if this information was leaked, it could spell Alice's end in the conclave...

"Rin, what do I do?!"

"Shhh! Calm down, Lady Alice." Rin pointed toward the bathroom. The queen was there. They couldn't let her overhear.

"It would be impossible for Lady Sisbell to know about the incidents between you two. Her astral powers only work within a thousand-foot radius."

And the Sovereignty and neutral city were several hundred miles apart. The possibility of Sisbell re-creating their meetings was close to none. Alice acquiesced, accepting Rin's opinion. But that didn't mean the situation had now turned for the better.

"...Maybe she overheard us?"

"It's possible."

She hadn't seen them share a meal or sit together at the opera. If she had seen anything, it would have been Alice and Rin talking in the Sovereignty. There was a chance Sisbell had begun to be suspicious about the boy who had come up in their discussions.

"We must put a stop to this quickly...," the attendant suggested in a hushed voice. "I believe Lady Sisbell must find this shady...and suspect you have been colluding with the Empire."

"N-no way!" Alice sat down on Sisbell's bed in place of a chair. "I *do* know Iska, but that's because we're enemies on the battlefield. Any rumors about me sleeping with the Empire would be an embarrassment!"

"Yes, but this could be good for us. Lady Sisbell isn't in the Sovereignty."

"...Which means?"

"My queen!" Rin called into the bathroom. "We could not find any clues about Lady Sisbell's activities in her bedroom. But I have a proposal."

"...And what could that be?"

"I ask that you grant Lady Alice permission to go on an excursion."

The queen stepped into the room, exiting the bathroom.

Rin knelt and lowered her head. "I ask that you allow Lady Alice to go directly to the destination where Lady Sisbell has gone, to meet with her."

"Hmm?" The queen looked at Alice.

Rin eyed the princess in a way that must have meant something. "Yes, Lady Sisbell is in a foreign country. Because she cannot seclude herself in her room, she cannot hide any of her suspicious behavior."

"Why Alice?"

"Because they are siblings."

"..."

"Even if Lady Sisbell had something trivial to hide, she might have reservations opening up to a servant. After all, even the friendliest servant is still a stranger. But Lady Alice and Lady Sisbell are family."

Queen Mirabella could not leave the royal palace. Elletear had just returned, which meant it would be unfair to send her off on another trip. Through the process of elimination, Alice was the optimal choice.

"I have heard Lady Sisbell has no guard."

"Yes, she is letting her keeper handle everything."

"Lady Alice would be able to protect Lady Sisbell."

"...However, Rin, we don't even know where Salinger is. What is your plan for him?" Her worry was apparent in her eyes. "He must be hiding within our country. If he comes to attack the royal palace, we would need Alice to deter him. I don't think it's wise to have her leave in this situation."

"The sorcerer is injured." The attendant did not miss a beat. "And not in a way that he can make a complete recovery within a few days. While Lady Alice is absent, I can assure you that he will not be prioritizing attacking this place."

"..."

"My queen."

"I understand."

It took a moment for Nebulis IIX to sigh. She was reluctant, but she had no other proposal.

"I will go along with your plan. Alice, I will grant you permission to leave."

"Yes, Mother."

Nice thinking, Rin! Alice was cheering in her heart for the kneeling attendant.

Now she had a pretext for following her sister. She would be able to talk to Sisbell, just between the two of them.

...That's right. I'm sure it was all a mistake... She's misunderstood the nature of my relationship with Iska.

She couldn't have anyone thinking that a princess of the Nebulis Sovereignty had any ties to an Imperial soldier. She needed to go after her and immediately correct the misunderstanding.

"Mother, don't worry. I will be back within four days."

The round trip took three days.

She would give herself a whole day to talk to Sisbell. This time, she wouldn't let her sister run away. If her sister did, Alice would grab her by the scruff of the neck and talk to her.

"Rin, make arrangements immediately!"

Alice lightly let her royal dress billow as she stormed out of Sisbell's room.

...Sisbell... What are you doing right now? And where?

Her mind started to churn.

CHAPTER 4

Unit 907

1

The independent state of Alsamira. Surrounded by the desert, the resort town had been enveloped by night as most guests headed to bed.

"It's been a year, Saint Disciple Iska."

On the hotel's fourth floor, the blond girl had snuck into Iska's room, speaking very calmly from her pinned-down position on the floor.

"Do you remember me?"

"...You're..."

His clearest memory of her had been from the afternoon.

It was the exact same girl who had bumped into him from behind at the intersection. He had been on the road where they had carried Captain Mismis after she had tuckered herself out from playing in the pool.

But they had first met a year ago.

* * *

"We're enemies."

"But you're letting me go?"

"...You're the one from the jail...?"

"My name is Sisbell. I am honored you remember me." On her back, she offered a small smile.

A year ago, he wouldn't have thought the girl imprisoned for being a witch was beautiful by any standards.

...Her clothes and hair were a mess... Even though she was smaller than I am, she was still trying to stand up to me.

She seemed like an entirely different person now.

Taken by curiosity, her large eyes were looking intently back at him with her mesmerizing face. Her glossy strawberry blond hair spread across the carpet. Her dress was simple yet cultured.

...Why did she sneak into my room? ...I don't think it'd be easy to get a key. How did she even find out my room number?

His thoughts went in circles.

"I apologize for forcing my way into your room so late at night...but...um..."

The girl was still on the ground. Her face was slightly flushed, and she turned away from Iska, who was looking straight at her.

"I'm...not used to being treated in this manner..."

"What?"

"...If you wouldn't mind getting off me, I would be so happy."

He had pinned down a dainty girl, leaning over her. When he finally realized that, Iska leaped up.

"Oh, s-sorry! ...But it's not what you think. When I heard the door open, I thought it was a thief sneaking in—"

"No... It's fine... I was the one in the wrong." The blond girl got up, her face red.

CHAPTER 4

She brushed off the dust on her dress with her hands, giving him a passing glance before sitting on the sofa. Every action was hypnotizing. There was no way around not staring.

She was lovely.

And she had to have been born into royalty or nobility and received years of vigorous training if she moved with such grace.

...Come to think of it, Alice is the same... She moved with poise when we were in the hotel together...

He knew it was off that he was reminded of Alice from Sisbell's actions and appearance.

"May I call you Iska?"

He snapped back to his senses, standing in surprise.

The ephemeral girl carefully observed him. He nodded silently to her.

"Iska. I apologize for two of my deplorable actions. First, I forced my way into your room with a spare key, but most importantly..."

She took a breath.

"When you let me out of the prison, I did not give you a word of thanks. Though it was rude of me...I was afraid it was a trap at the time. I did not think that anyone from the Empire would let me free."

"I think that's natural. I knew I was doing something ridiculous, too."

Iska nodded where he was still standing in the living room. He elected not to sit on the sofa. He didn't know anything about Sisbell's abilities. If she attacked him with astral power from the front, Iska wasn't confident he could react in time.

He had saved this witch. At the same time, that didn't mean she was his ally, and it was still possible she could turn on him.

"I will pay you back here."

She had a blue crystal bracelet, reverently holding it out after

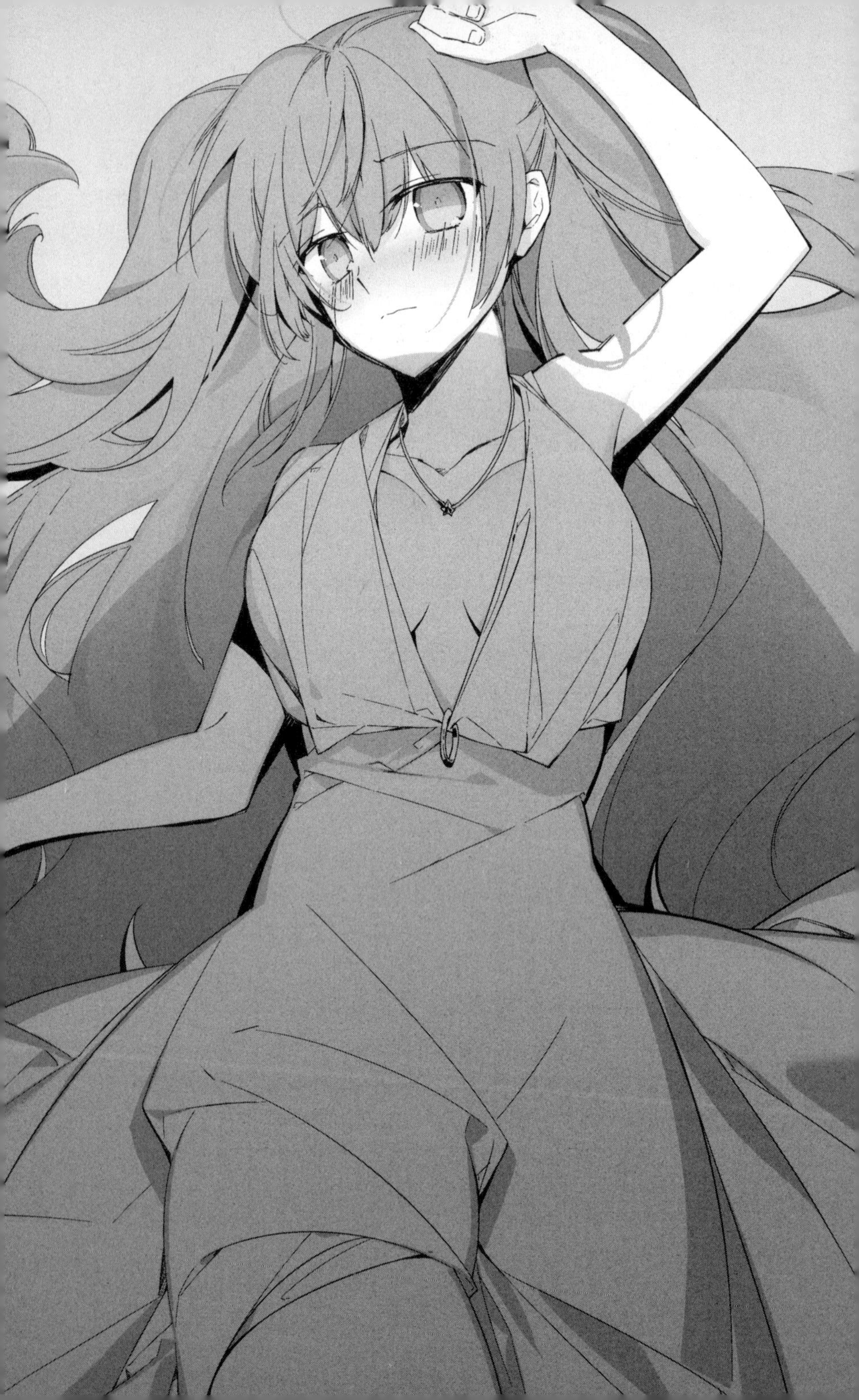

having tugging it off her own left wrist. "It is a later piece by the jewel craftsman Bildred Morpheus. It represents the works of early last century. It's not just beautiful. It has historical value. In every gemstone shop around the world, even if they low-balled you, it would still get you a mansion and—"

"W-wait a sec!" Iska shouted as she held the bracelet out in front of his eyes. "What's going on…?"

"Like I said, a token of thanks for saving me." The witch had the bracelet resting in both her hands.

Iska gently pushed back her hands, which were pale as though they had never been burned by the sun.

"I can't take this."

"Why not?"

"That's not why I saved you. I wouldn't have done it if I wanted compensation. And there's no way to get back my position as a Saint Disciple with money."

"…" Her lips pursed.

"Headquarters have their eyes on me now. If I accept something from you, they'll definitely think I'm working with the Sovereignty."

"I took that into account."

"What?"

"I came here in order to invite you to our country."

Sisbell's eyes were sincere. Standing up, she put her hand on her chest.

"This past year, I've investigated you. Everyone in the neutral city knows about the incident that happened while you were under the direct command of the throne."

"…So that's how you knew my name?"

"Yes," she answered with a soft smile. "You lost your position as a Saint Disciple. I don't think it would be an exaggeration to say your reputation has fallen. It is my turn to pay you back. I can promise you status and prestige, even greater than before. The Sovereignty would warmly welcome you."

"..."

"I will guarantee a position for you and your safety. Even though you come from the Empire, there will be no issues with your livelihood."

This was like déjà vu.

In the wastelands, the Ice Calamity Witch, Princess Alice, had made the same proposal to him as red dust billowed around them.

"You. Become my subordinate.
"I will secure you a position. You'll become a refugee of the Empire."

Did that mean the girl in front of his eyes had influence that rivaled Alice's? He couldn't imagine there were many in a country with political power to rival a princess.

"Who...?"

"Yes?"

"Who are you?"

Was she related to Alice?

Iska gripped his hands into fists and stopped himself from saying anything more. Asking questions related to Alice was off the table. If he asked anything, Sisbell would suspect he had a relationship with Alice.

...If headquarters catches wind of this...I might actually be executed on the spot.

"It wouldn't be so easy to prepare a position equal to a Saint Disciple."

"I could do it," she assured. "I have access to the royal family... as their *attendant*."

CHAPTER 4

"So you're close to them?"

"Yes. I am in a position close to the royal family. I have received permission from my employers to do this. I can assure you."

She was an envoy of the royal family.

In other words, she bore a close relationship to someone who was familiar with the queen herself. That was why it was possible for her to make a proposal on par with Alice's.

"Do you understand what I'm trying to say?"

"...Why me?" He turned to Sisbell, who was blushing red. Iska gulped. "I won't deny you're close to the royal family. I think it must be true, but I'm sure there are others who could fill this position."

"Uh." Her shoulders shot up.

"The astral corps can mobilize at a single command. Even an Imperial soldier knows that the royal family has guards," Iska said.

"..."

"Are you inviting me to the Sovereignty because you want someone from the Empire?"

There was a shadow...of sorrow that had made its way into her eyes.

Since Iska had hit the bull's-eye, she had been at a loss for how to answer. From the way she quivered and bit her lip, she almost looked as though she was desperately holding back tears.

"...But...it's because I...," the blond girl managed to rasp out, "I have no servants. I can't trust anyone..."

"What?"

"I can't tell you the specifics right now. But...the Sovereignty isn't as much of a monolith as it seems to other countries."

"...But what does that have to do with not having any servants?"

Wasn't that an exaggeration? Iska didn't want to accuse her of lying, but he didn't think that would apply to the one princess he knew.

"I *can't trust anyone!*" Her voice echoed through the living room.

She stepped up in front of Iska without giving him a chance to say anything as she took his hand and squeezed it.

"I can't trust anyone in the country. That's why I need to ask you... I need someone to become a knight and protect me in place of a servant!"

"..."

"If that weren't the case, I wouldn't have come by myself to ask you to do this. I'm weak, after all... To present myself to a frightening Imperial soldier, a former Saint Disciple... Do you understand how much preparation it takes to expose oneself alone in this situation...?!"

At the end, she was practically shrieking, mixed with violent sobs.

"Even when I came into your room, I was genuinely terrified that you might shoot me, thinking I was a thief... I don't have strong astral powers like my mother and—"

Like her mother?

She immediately realized the suspicion wordlessly floating into Iska's mind. She finally noticed that she had been talking, swayed by her emotions, without a pause.

"...I'm sorry. I lost my composure." A weak sigh escaped from her.

The witch reluctantly let go of Iska's hand.

"I can't believe, out of all the things I could have done, I let myself ramble when I was making a request of you... I have no negotiation skills. Please don't get the wrong idea. I just wanted to rely on you, and I got worked up..."

"—"

"I'd like to do this over again. I'm glad I met you today..."

CHAPTER 4

The girl named Sisbell turned around.

It was as though she were flowing in water. Her fluid gait made her fair hair fan out as she left Iska's room behind.

Click. The door locked automatically. Beyond the thick door, her footsteps became fainter until he finally could not hear them.

"What was up with that...?"

She had left him behind. Iska sighed in surprise. He had come visiting a desert far from the Empire and Sovereignty...and yet, he had somehow met the girl who he had broken out of prison a year ago.

...Is it a coincidence? No, but...she knew what my room number was. How did she figure that out?

He could switch rooms just to feel safe. In any case, he probably needed to check for a bug. He looked around the living room.

"Oh."

His eyes stopped on the sofa where the girl had been sitting.

"She got me..."

It was the blue crystal bracelet—the one that Iska had already turned down. Sisbell had unashamedly left it behind when she had stood up from the sofa.

—*I won't give up*, it seemed to symbolize in her place.

He picked it up. After carefully checking whether it was bugged, Iska turned his head to face the heavens.

"Who is she...?"

The shop streets were illuminated by neon lights.

The freezing winds of the desert whistled through the main thoroughfare as Sisbell ran as fast as her legs would take her.

"...What...? What do you think you're doing, Sisbell?!"

She had figured out where Iska was staying, sneaking into his room and finally reaching the point where she could negotiate with him.

Then why?

"This isn't like me...!"

How many years had it been since she had raised her voice?

She had never complained to her mother—not even once. At most, when she was a child, she had been stubborn to her poor keeper, but that was the extent of her experiences.

"This is a disgrace. Even after I practiced all the scenarios..."

She had wanted to get closer to the former Saint Disciple Iska.

Sisbell had secretly felt confident when it came to smooth negotiations. Despite her appearance, she had picked up her mother's techniques while she was young.

Which smile did she weaponize? What kind of tone was necessary?

What did she need to do to make him lower his guard and win him over? She had wanted to pull him over to her side. She had been confident she could. There was just one thing that had been outside her calculations.

Iska was *too nice* of a boy.

How could she have guessed?

How could she have guessed he would have accepted her?

"...*If you wouldn't mind getting off me, I would be so happy.*"

"Oh, s–sorry!"

Sisbell had been the one who had forced her way into his room. What kind of person would apologize to someone who was breaking and entering? That had bothered her from the get-go.

CHAPTER 4

His words didn't indicate he was an Imperial citizen who feared witches. He had treated her like another human being.

And that was specifically why Sisbell's emotions had come undone.

With him…she could open up about her true feelings. Even if she yelled and begged for his help, he would have been okay with her.

For a moment, Sisbell forgot her own circumstances and started yelling.

"…What a disgrace!" She chewed on her bottom lip, repeating that phrase.

She pulled a communications device out of her pocket.

"My lady?"

"Shuvalts, it's me… Yes… Uh-huh. That's right. All we did was meet tonight," she said to her keeper, who was awaiting orders at the hotel. "I will try again. I'll wait for another opportunity. You're right. I mustn't rush things. I will definitely make sure I succeed. I won't give up."

Her mother's life was on the line.

To protect her mother from that *monster* that hid in the royal family, she would need a strong ally.

2

The sun rose over the sandy horizon.

The frosty grains of sand started to absorb the heat, and the independent state of Alsamira began to blister.

It was enough to make anyone sweat, which was instantly evaporated by the desert winds.

"Time for barbecuuuue!" Captain Mismis boomed, as passionate as these sweltering winds.

There was a camping area immediately within walking distance of the hotel. Like the pool, this popular establishment was emblematic of the resort, which meant it was flooded with tourists from the early morning.

"This is paradise! I can't believe I get to eat barbecue for breakfast. While we were in the capital, I didn't even have time to toast bread. I only ate canned stuff." The commander held a perfectly chilled drink can in her right hand.

As she gulped it down, the winds whipped against her. It had to be delicious.

"I'm so blessed…"

"If you have enough time to get drunk, help us, boss."

Jhin was keeping track of the gas burner's flame. Next to him, Nene was slicing up vegetables, and Iska was in the middle of cutting the meat.

"I'll cook the meat!"

"Oh, Captain. We need to put the veggies on first, since they won't heat up as fast. Here!"

"Boo." The captain slumped over when Nene pushed a plate piled with vegetables toward her.

"…" Iska kept an eye on the captain, even as he intently observed the waves of people coming in and out of the camp area. Most of them came with their families. The others were couples or old married pairs of two. Even though his gaze pierced through the crowd, he couldn't find Sisbell from the other night.

…It just happened yesterday… I thought she would have followed me to the campgrounds, but I guess not.

He didn't know whether to tell the others. Iska had taken the

CHAPTER 4

whole night to think about the decision, balancing the advantages and disadvantages of his choice.

If he came clean, they would be informed about the risk of an astral mage nearby.

But if he tried talking about Sisbell, he would end up having to divulge details about the incident from a year before.

After a long night of deliberation, Iska decided he wouldn't tell them *yet*.

...It would be easy to tell them. I can do it whenever I want... But once I act on it, I can't take it back.

If he shared the information about the incident of breaking a witch out of jail, he was worried his friends could be suspected of involvement. They could all be thrown in jail on the whims of the Eight Great Apostles or headquarters.

And they were in an independent state.

They were all aware of the risk of staying near an astral mage from the Sovereignty, who had come to this resort for their own reasons. They were prepared for the minute chance that one might attack. The three of them knew of the possibility that they might encounter a witch, even if he didn't immediately tell them about Sisbell.

"Aha! I know, Iska! It just came to me!"

"Whoa?!"

The captain hopped right in front of him, grinning suspiciously. Could she have read his mind? He backed away when he saw Captain Mismis's pointed look.

"Wh-what?"

"Iska, you were looking there, huh? Ta-da! Roasted sausages. I put some special spices on them! Eat up!"

"..."

"Huh? What's wrong?"

"...Nothing. I just realized I didn't need to worry about some stuff that's been on my mind."

Captain Mismis didn't find anything off about Iska's response, holding a plate of roasted sausages out to him.

"Okay, hurry, Iska. Try one."

"Are you sure you want me to be the taste tester? You're the one who was looking forward to this barbecue."

"It's fine. They're super spicy."

"What?"

"And an opportunity arises!" Mismis shouted, stuffing it right into his open mouth.

Iska immediately felt as though he'd been struck by lightning. With one bite, his tongue was on fire.

"Nhhhhhh! These are so spicy! Ow!"

"Iska! Water! Drink some water!" shouted Nene.

He tried to wash it away with cold water, but the burning sensation lingered.

"Wow. Specialty spices from the desert don't disappoint. Looks like the rumors were true. Your tongue gets all swollen, and you feel like you've been electrocuted."

"Please don't make me your lab rat!"

"Ha-ha. It's rated X for spiciness, and I thought you could take it, Iska. Anyway, can I have everyone's attention?"

There were four sausages roasting over the flame grill. They were browned and smelled delicious.

"There's one special sausage in the mix! Rated Double-X for spiciness! Which means it's twice as spicy as Iska's sausage. Time for a little game of Russian roulette!"

Iska, Jhin, and Nene looked at one another. Captain Mismis,

the proposer of this evil game, was the only one with expectant eyes.

"But wait, there's more! If you're the one who eats that sausage, you'll receive another punishment! You'll have to be the one to eat all the vegetables here!"

"...So that's what you're after."

"...You just don't want to eat your vegetables."

"...Hey, Captain. It's not exactly healthy to only eat meat all the time."

"You've all got it wrong! I'd like to eat my veggies, too! But I think the occasion calls for a fun little competition! And I won't be the one to stop it!"

Everything about her expression screamed that she was heartbroken. Not that she could hide the excitement in her voice.

"But there is one saving grace for the person who eats the super-spicy sausage. If they can pretend it's not them, they won't get the other punishment."

"So you would need to eat the whole thing without changing your expression?" Jhin downed some ice-cold juice. "Is it actually possible to hide it, Iska?"

"No way." Iska decisively shook his head. "It's like a bomb went off in my mouth."

"Cool. But, Captain, I'm going to warn you: If *you* get the spicy one, you'll have to eat all the vegetables. And we won't let you have a single piece of meat."

"Oh-ho? That's what I should be saying to you. All right! Players, fight!"

They each reached out to one of the four sausages on top of the grill and took a big bite.

...This...is fine. It's a normal sausage. I didn't get the spicy one!

Now the only ones that were left were the other three.

Nene took a wary bite of hers. Captain Mismis eagerly bit off a chunk. Jhin had already polished off his sausage.

"H-huh? Who got the spicy one?" Captain Mismis blinked. "I'm sure it was Nene!"

"I-it wasn't me! You're acting suspicious, Captain Mismis, especially since you accused me!"

"But it wasn't me, either. But Iska and Jhin seem fine…"

"I know. Maybe the captain forgot to put in the spicy sausage, so we all had normal ones?"

"Hmm…m-maybe?"

Nene and Captain Mismis seemed puzzled.

Jhin nonchalantly confessed, "It was me." Jhin, of all people.

"I finished without any of you figuring it out, so I guess we have to keep the game going."

"No way?! You, Jhin?!" Mismis exclaimed.

"Whoa! Hey, how'd you pull it off?!" Nene asked.

"With ice." The silver-haired sniper was holding a bottle of juice with ice. "I cooled off the inside of my mouth. With a numb tongue, I couldn't taste or feel anything."

"Unfair, Jhin!" cried Mismis.

"I just happened to drink some of my juice before we started. I didn't break any rules… *Cough!* …Ah, shit. After all that, it's still… *Cough…!*"

"Jhin?!" Nene yelped.

"…These spices are…totally not normal… I can't believe it'd be this strong after I cooled down my mouth…"

Jhin was bright red. When Iska and Nene saw his face, they knew…this wasn't something that could be withstood.

"Anyway, I got through it, so we're going to keep going with the game."

CHAPTER 4

"Ugh… I-in that case, you can't use that strategy anymore!"

The captain pulled out additional sausages from the cooler. As they roasted over the open flame, they started to smell good again.

"This is rated Triple-X! It's the ultimate delicacy! It even has an age-limit warning for anyone under fifteen! You won't be able to handle this with your strategies, Jhin!"

"A-are you doing okay, Captain…?"

"I don't want to eat the vegetables!"

"Did you just…?! I knew it was because you were a picky eater!"

The first round was just to get things going. She had been initially scared that she might end up getting the sausage, but when she confirmed Jhin had been the target, she was certain: Luck was on her side today.

They could see right through her.

"Okay. The final match. We're going to settle things for good!"

All four of the sausages appeared to be identical.

They each forked a sausage and held their breaths as they took bites.

…Hmm? …It's fine. I didn't get the spicy one!

Iska hadn't been able to withstand the sausage rated X for spiciness.

Jhin had taken the perfect countermeasure, but he hadn't been able to endure one with Double-X.

When it came to the Triple-X level of spiciness, no one would be able to hide their reaction. It would immediately show on their face.

"Not mine," Iska said.

"Me neither. What about you, Jhin?" Nene asked.

"Like I'd let myself get it twice in a row."

Three pairs of eyes naturally gathered on their captain.

"Hey, Captain Mismis… Oh." Nene stopped talking.

The commander was locked in place with the sausage in her mouth.

"...You, huh?"

"―――――――――――" She didn't answer.

Her face was as red as a ripe apple. Then it paled. Her face turned sheet white as though she had burned right out.

"...*Bwoof.*" Captain Mismis barked like a puppy, collapsing on the spot.

"Captain?!"

"O-oh no! This is bad, Iska. Hurry! We need to get her water! Or an ambulance!"

"I'm just so done with this. I have nothing to say."

They lugged their incapacitated captain over to the shade.

She really was the furthest from an actual adult. After they looked down at her, all three of them turned up to the heavens for mercy.

3

In the eastern part of the continent. The yellow deserts of Route Herald.

The sandy wasteland enclosed the independent state of Alsamira. It currently served as a safe route, but it had once been known to be a land where its many victims never came home.

"*This route was established because the survey units risked their lives ascertaining the territory of the basilisks,*" explained one of the bus crew in a large loop bus that carried tourists to Alsamira.

"*The animals inhabiting these harsh lands evolved to become stronger to ensure the survival of their species. As you all know, the top of the ecosystem is the large wandering beast known as the basilisk.*"

CHAPTER 4

According to legend, it could turn people to stone with its eyes.

...I've heard those who manage to escape are covered in sand... which is how these legends started.

They needed to be vigilant about its ferocity.

Even at nearly four yards in length, it was terrifyingly nimble and vindictive. A basilisk would never allow anyone to step in its nest. There had been records of people being followed all the way to the ends of the desert after committing this crime.

"But you have nothing to worry about. This bus makes detours around all basilisk nests. Even if we encounter one, we are equipped with tear gas containing chemicals that the basilisks hate. There are even two specialist hunters on board who—"

"We're relying on you," Alice answered in a monotone as she leaned onto the window frame.

She had gone by way of the neutral city on her solitary trip. She had transferred over to a loop bus from the closest city to the desert of Route Herald and then continued to ride for another ten hours.

...I'm sick of seeing the desert... And sitting for so long is doing a number on my butt. And my shoulders feel stiff because I can't move around much.

Most importantly, Rin wasn't with her. Alice was plagued by the anxiety of going on a trip without an attendant and the boredom from a lack of conversation partner. They were both emotions that Alice hadn't felt in so long that she'd almost forgotten what they felt like.

"I guess it's been about ten years? The last time was when my mother took me out with her on the locomotive."

They had been on a continental railway at night.

Her memories of traveling across the country by railway while accompanied by the royal palace retainers came back to her. Alice had been riding on a railcar heading in the direction of the burning lights in the neutral city. She still remembered when she had been attacked by the group of roving beasts that kept that land as part of their territory.

...I wonder what got into me back then.

...When I saw those gigantic beasts for the first time, I guess I must have been frightened.

Her body had frozen in place. Even with her astral powers, Alice still hadn't had full mastery over them as a young girl, scampering away in fear at the back of the train when faced with the group of beasts.

"I remember that happened..."

It was similar to this situation. The only difference was that present-day Alice wouldn't be frightened if she encountered a basilisk. Of course, she would prefer to avoid the nest of a beast if possible.

"Watch out!" the driver yelled.

The bus driver suddenly hit the brakes, jerking to a stop from chugging up a sand dune. It dug up a mound of sand as it screeched to a halt. Even Alice felt herself almost launched out of her seat from the recoil.

"Wh-what is going on...? That could have been dangerous."

It seemed like some passengers had hit their bodies on impact. The inside of the bus became slightly panicked.

"W-we sincerely apologize... Uh, um..."

"We have found *prints* ahead of us," muttered the operator, causing the passengers to stir.

Ahead of the bus were curious tracks appearing along the gentle slope of sand. There were traces that something gigantic had been crossing the desert.

"Hmm? That's...!" Alice stood up from her seat, sprinting over to the back door of the bus and manually forcing the door open.

CHAPTER 4

"M-miss?! It's dangerous out there! You can't go outside—"

She broke through the cabin crew as they tried to restrain her. She was on top of the hot sand. Grains of grit whipped around her. Just one step outside made her start sweating immediately. The scorching winds buffeted her. Alice started dashing down the dune, following the tracks on the sand.

They were footprints, traces of something much larger than a human lurking in the desert.

...A basilisk? But we're far away from any nests... Plus, would it leave clear footprints?

The traces were bipedal. A basilisk slithered over the sand to travel with its peculiar movements, making prints like someone skating on ice.

What did that mean when it came to these footprints?

An elephant or rhinoceros must have left these heavy tracks while walloping and swaying over the ground.

"Is it bigger than a basilisk?"

She felt chills run down her spine. The basilisk should have been the king of this desert's ecosystem. If that was the case, what had created these huge footprints?

"..." Alice noticed the black splotches in and between the tracks.

Is this...blood? When she approached it, her nose was tickled by a faint odor. It wasn't blood. The malodor that lingered in her nostrils and polluted lungs was—

"Machine oil?"

It brought back memories of her battles with the Imperial soldiers. Even the Imperial bases that Alice had targeted were always permeated with a similar smell.

"...And it's headed toward..."

The footprints went off to the east, continuing toward the

independent state of Alsamira. Based on the pristine condition of the tracks, it hadn't been long since it had passed through.

"I was hoping this would be a good opportunity to talk to my sister, but prospects are looking bleak…"

The wind blowing through the dune swept up her golden hair like so many silk threads. She held it down to keep it out of her eyes.

"I hope I can reach it today." Alice shook her head slightly.

4

Within the suburbs of Alsamira was the residential district, neatly lined with wealthy villas—far from the pools, campgrounds, and shopping areas around the hotels.

It was quiet there.

Past its outstretched roads were desert paths that led to the horizon.

"Hey…Iska, are we at the hotel yet? I'm so tired. I can't walk anymore," Mismis complained.

"It's just ahead."

"We could have stayed another night at the other hotel…"

The captain stalked forward while Nene and Iska held her hands.

"I can't believe you'd change our hotel. You're so cautious, Iska."

"I'm just trying to save on our budget. Hotels near the shopping streets are all pricey. This hotel has comparable reviews as the one from yesterday, but it's way cheaper."

"I remember informing you before we left," Jhin reminded, walking behind everyone with hands full of Captain Mismis's swimming ring and other miscellaneous luggage.

CHAPTER 4

They had been causing a ruckus since the barbecue that morning.

After that, they had swum in the same pool as the day before. They were finally on their way back home. But at Iska's suggestion, they had changed hotels.

He had done it on the pretext of the residential district hotels being cheaper.

...But Captain Mismis is right for once... I'm changing hotels because I am cautious.

The night before, Sisbell had visited him. The incident had blown over quietly, but when he thought about what would have happened if it had been an attack by the astral corps, it sent a shiver down his spine.

It wasn't just that he would be in danger. His friends would be involved, too.

...I chose the hotel arbitrarily... I just called in to book it. She shouldn't be able to figure it out.

No one was trailing them, either.

Until he had come here, Iska had always kept a watchful eye on his surroundings. He was sure that there weren't any Sovereign assassins dressed as normal people.

"Ah, I'm blessed," Mismis said, seemingly to herself. "It's been a while since I had so much fun," quietly admitted the captain with blue hair. "Nights can suck on normal holidays... I end up thinking about heading off to the battlefield when morning comes. But right now, I'm excited about our fun schedule tomorrow. Just thinking about it makes me feel happy."

"I'm glad you want to have fun, but make sure you've got enough energy left to walk on your own two legs."

"Fiiine." Captain Mismis smiled innocently as she gripped Iska's and Nene's arms.

That was when Nene suddenly stopped in a fluster, yanking on the captain's left arm. "Oh, wait. Stop for a sec, Captain."

"What?"

"It's *come off.*"

A faint green light illuminated through her thin shirt. The radiant light was coming from Mismis's left shoulder.

"Oh! I-I'm so sorry, Nene! I didn't notice…"

"It's fine. The end of the bandage just curled up. I think it must have happened while you were swimming in the pool."

She flipped up Mismis's sleeve and reapplied the bandage. In that time, Mismis's smile had faded.

"R-right… I shouldn't be out having fun. I need to figure out a way to hide this mark."

"You'll be no help. You might as well have fun."

"Jhin! You meanie!"

"Iska, Nene, and I couldn't figure anything out. It'd be better if we clear our heads for a while and then start thinking up ideas from scratch. We still have that sixty-day extension."

The sun was setting. The sniper watched the horizon steeped in crimson and suddenly narrowed his eyes.

"Well, if you're worried about it, boss, let's go to a general market tomorrow."

"A general market? Like the one happening in the back of the roads?"

"This is an independent state. Because it's not the Empire or the Sovereignty, *they can import stuff from either side.* It's basically a black market."

There were Imperial guns and bullets and Sovereign fibers woven with special metals and worn by the astral corps. The source country was unknown and unofficial. Of course, prices were high due to the exclusivity of the goods sold.

CHAPTER 4

"The general rule of the market is that the early birds are the winners. If we're going to get anything, we need to be there first thing in the morning."

"Jhin, are you saying we're going to get…that? Um, that thing from back when the captain was taken hostage at the vortex…?" Nene asked.

"Yeah, the bandage on the former commander Shanorotte."

"Did this surprise you?"
"Y-you're a witch?! O-ow!"
"That's right. I'm what you call a witch."

The former commander Shanorotte had disguised herself as part of the Imperial Army. She had ripped off the bandage—which hid her astral crest and energy. The stuff on Captain Mismis's shoulder was just medical tape, which meant it didn't block her powers, though the mark was unseen to the eye.

"When it comes to researching astral power, they've progressed more than the Empire—according to the former commander Shanorotte."

The Sovereignty had developed a special textile that could block astral energy. That didn't exist within Imperial territories.

"It's fine if all we can get is a knockoff. We'll get our hands on the stuff that was developed in the Sovereignty—even if it's just the instruction manual."

"Of course, Jhin! This makes me happy. You have the biggest potty mouth, but you can be so reliable when things get rough!"

"Get off me. It's already sweltering."

"What happened to your nice side?! Hey!"

Jhin nimbly sidestepped the captain as she tried to embrace him.

"…Hey. A girl is offering to give you a hug! You're so antisocial."

"Captain, I can see the place where we're staying."

Patting her small back, Iska pointed at the hotel along the road. Compared to the luxury hotels, it didn't look as nice, but the reviews weren't bad.

Most importantly, this hotel was owned by the Empire. Anyone related to the Nebulis Sovereignty would think twice about trying to break into it.

"Captain, Jhin, pick up the pace!" encouraged Nene.

They were at the automatic door, which was basked in blinding light. As they all turned to look back at Iska in the lobby, he gripped his Imperial weapon. This was outside of Imperial domain. Unless one had the common worldwide currency, it wouldn't be possible to pay for their stay.

"It'd be bad if the money exchange closed. I'm going to go there right now."

"Okay. But come back soon, Iska. We're heading straight to dinner after this."

"Got it." Holding his money, he hurried outside.

It was evening. The sun was already more than halfway below the desert horizon.

"Let's see—"

He left the other three and headed out of the hotel. He had pretended to go inside the hotel and immediately ran back over to the road outside.

...I'll make them think I went into the hotel and tail them.

...We'll run into each other here.

He had purposefully chosen a hotel in the quiet residential district because there weren't as many passersby. If anyone was walking along the sidewalks, they would catch his eye. But he didn't see anyone suspicious.

"...Guess she's not here."

CHAPTER 4

Sisbell had invaded his room with expertise, somehow managing to obtain Iska's hotel room number and a spare key from the hotel manager. He suspected the same might happen again that day…or the astral corps might pay him a visit in his room and—

Although he was hypervigilant, he didn't see anyone who caught his eye on the large street in front of the hotel.

"I knew she wouldn't come this far."

"Who?" A sweet voice giggled.

Impossible! Iska whipped around toward the hotel entrance. The glass automatic doors had parted to reveal a blond girl walking coolly out of the lobby.

Iska felt cold rather than surprise.

"Good evening, Iska. Were you looking for me?"

"…Did you use some kind of trick?"

It was unbelievable.

How had she come for him before he had even gotten to the hotel?

"I said I would redo things. I don't intend on giving up."

Her innocent smile immediately settled on a serious expression.

Sisbell was wearing a different dress, elegantly lifting the hem of her skirt once she was out the door.

"We're in the public eye. If we're seen together, it would spell bad news for both of us. Would you be open to changing locations?"

"I agree. But where?"

The day was growing dark already. It was too dim to talk at a corner of the building. And there could be witnesses. But the restaurants were busy with guests having dinner.

"Over there. You can see a large building on the horizon."

Sisbell was pointing in the direction of the shopping zone. Facing the desert was a big plot. He could see the shadow of a gigantic establishment that looked like a factory.

"That's…"

"A crude-oil mining facility. They open holes deep in the desert bed with drills to extract oil. According to rumors, the Empire has its eyes on its wealth of energy."

"You sure know a lot."

"That's because it's part of my duties here. Oh, I can't tell you any more details." The girl winked mischievously.

"Looks like we'll need to walk awhile."

"That's a good thing. We know there won't be as many people."

"…Okay. But let me tell my friends. I need to let them know it'll take a while for me to get back."

"Be my guest."

He called Captain Mismis. Sisbell observed him for the duration of their call before pointing toward the desert.

"Then let us go."

She started walking, her hair trailing after her in the cool wind.

The oil extraction facility had to be a twenty-minute walk on foot. Until they reached the outskirts of its plot, the blond girl was entirely silent.

And the night wore on.

The entrance warned them against trespassing. They passed by the sign, venturing farther into the plot.

"I think that we're far enough. It's empty at night, just like I thought."

Sisbell turned around.

Iska needed clarification on the shocking secret to her tricks.

"…From your astral power, huh?"

"What do you mean?"

CHAPTER 4

"I only decided to change hotels today, but you were waiting there ahead of time."

He had been thinking about it all the way here, though he couldn't pinpoint her exact skills.

"I was wondering about the spell you used."

"A spell? I didn't realize you were a jokester. Or do you think I'm a scary witch?" She gracefully placed her hands over her chest and looked up at him.

She had called herself a "witch."

"As you've guessed, it's related to my astral power."

The blond girl fiddled with the button at the front of her dress. She used her other hand to open it before moving down to another button.

Under the sunset, she started to expose her chest. This scene could have been a painting.

"Um! What're you…?"

"Don't fret. It isn't for nothing."

Under her collarbone was the faint glow of an astral crest that shone out of the gaps of the fabric.

"My astral power has the ability to reproduce the past, like a projector."

"Like footage?"

"I reproduced it all from this afternoon—when you called this hotel, when you recited the room number, when you talked about what time you wanted to check in. I can reproduce everything in front of my eyes. That's how I learned about those things."

"…I never knew there was…," Iska trailed off.

It was the first time Iska had heard of it, but she certainly wouldn't have been able to get to the hotel ahead of him without something to that extent.

Sisbell spoke about it with nonchalance, but it had to have interfered with time and space. Even among the many types of astral powers, it was a particularly rare one.

...It doesn't even compare to being tailed. This is diabolical. Nothing would be better for gathering intelligence.

If this witch snuck into the capital, she would strip down all manner of secret information, including intel from the organization headquarters, votes in the Imperial Senate, and profiles of all the Saint Disciples and Eight Great Apostles.

"Yesterday, I told you one lie—about my identity."

"Did you lie about your name being Sisbell? Or that you're an attendant of the royal family?"

"It's the latter. I'm—"

Her buttons remained open. She placed a hand on her radiant crest.

"I am Sisbell Lou Nebulis IX, a candidate to be the next queen."

"What?!"

"Although I don't have any proof to show you on this trip."

"..."

"Do you find it impossible to believe?"

"...The opposite." Iska shook his head, smiling painfully. His intuition hadn't been wrong—not when it came to the identity of this girl, who resembled the Ice Calamity Witch Aliceliese.

...A daughter of the queen. Like Alice...which means she's Alice's sister!

In that case, he could accept her powers. She was one of the Founder's descendants, one of the mages they called purebreds.

"I'll believe you're telling the truth. That's why I was so surprised... But are you sure about this? I *am* an Imperial soldier, after all."

"I want to bring an Imperial soldier on my side. That's why I used my trump card for this."

CHAPTER 4

Princess Sisbell's lips were trembling slightly. She didn't know when the Imperial soldier might change his mind and attack her with the knowledge that she was royalty.

"I have no allies, even though I am a princess."

"..." He tried to guess what that meant. "Is it because everyone is scared of your astral power?"

"Well, they consider me a nuisance. I can't reveal particulars, but our queen is being targeted…by one of the Founder's descendants."

"Huh?"

"Do you think that will lead to the self-destruction of the Sovereignty? The individual isn't attempting to steal the Sovereignty. They are seeking to do something even more catastrophic—the collapse and decline of the world itself. Once they have taken the queen's life, I am willing to bet they will strike the Empire."

"…Isn't that the same as suicide? Why would they do that?"

"To eliminate anyone who could get in their way within the Sovereignty. I believe they will try to involve all the powerful members of the royal family in the war to wipe out everyone."

But they could not hide that plot from Sisbell Lou Nebulis IX. Her astral powers could see through all plans.

"Which means you're being targeted, too? By the traitors trying to kill the queen?"

Princess Sisbell had no answer to offer. Her large eyes were full of fear.

"Just as I keep an eye on the traitor, they are observing me, too. I still don't know who is part of this scheme…"

Because of that, she couldn't rely on anyone in the Sovereignty. That was because she couldn't know if they were traitors.

"My powers are useless in battle… If you were to point a gun at me, my life would be over." She smiled in self-derision.

Her sweet face crumpled as the purebred bit her lip.

"Iska, I want you!" she yelled, which echoed pitifully through the desolate establishment.

"I am already prepared to welcome you, your family, and your unit as state guests. I will guarantee absolute safety. All you need to do is stay by my side. I want you to protect my life!"

"—"

"If the queen falls at the hands of the monster, the country will become its puppet. It will break out into total war with the Empire. If that happens, those you hold dear might perish," predicted the witch who could see into the past.

A full-blown war between the Empire and Nebulis Sovereignty wasn't far off. None of that seemed insincere to his ears.

"Iska, do you seek destruction? One of the two countries will annihilate the other, and the victor will lose its power and entirely decline. Is that the future you want?"

"...No."

"I want you to help me change it." Her cheeks must have been flushed from passion.

The princess of the Nebulis Sovereignty stepped forward.

"I won't ask you to betray the Empire. Three years... Even two would do just fine. You only need to be my guard until I become the next queen. After that, you may go back to the Empire or live in the Sovereignty. You could even escape the war and live in a neutral city."

"...I didn't expect this proposal. I feel like you're almost wasting this on me, honestly."

"Do you understand the situation?"

She took his response to be positive. The princess from the enemy nation seemed relieved as she offered her right hand.

"Then, Iska, I ask that you be my guard starting today."

"—"

CHAPTER 4

"Iska?"

"It is an unprecedented proposal, but I can't take your offer."

"What?" She gaped at him, unable to wrap her head around what was happening. Sisbell's eyes scanned him from the top of his head down to his toes. "I—I must have misheard."

"I have my reasons. I'm not fighting as an Imperial soldier for nothing."

"I can't. I can't stand on the Sovereignty's side."
"...And why would that be?"

And that was it.

This must have been the fate of this planet all along.

It was destiny for the Sovereign princess to make proposals and for him to turn them down. It was fate that their paths never converged.

"You were the one who said it. Do I want two countries to be annihilated? Of course not."

"Th-then why won't you join me?! At this rate, the Sovereignty will become a puppet nation, and we won't be able to avoid the two nations from going to war! To avoid this, we need to—"

"That's where we differ."

"What?"

"I hope to *end the strife between the two nations.*"

"How...how?"

"By negotiating for peace."

"That's impossible! There's no way that could ever happen!" she refused, enraged. "Even if I was to become queen, that is something that would never materialize. I believe our people...would never forgive the Empire."

"I realize that."

...I know... I've already heard that from Alice.

But had Iska faltered with this knowledge? No.

A full-blown war might be upon them.

Bring it on. That meant it was time to *stop the battle before it broke out.* That was Iska's goal, and that was what separated his ideals from Alice's and Sisbell's motives.

"That's why I can't be your follower."

"...But..." The blond girl staggered. Just as she seemed as though she was about to stumble to her knees, she leaned against a streetlight and desperately stopped herself. She had been worn down. "—Uh...ugh..."

Her delicate shoulders quivered. A faint sob escaped from her. She ground her teeth, trying to bear through it, but it overflowed from between her gritted teeth.

"......So...I really have no allies......," she mumbled, as though she was coughing up blood.

"That's too bad. I am disappointed, Sisbell."

The reply seemed to come from nowhere in particular. Someone was behind them.

"A young girl's tears spilling in the cold night. How poetic. It could be a painting. Or is that a part of your act to gain sympathy from an Imperial soldier?"

A man in black wearing a mask appeared under the streetlight...followed by an armed group of four. They were wearing pilot suits made from hides that looked out of place in a resort, and their faces were concealed by helmets.

"Well, Sisbell. It seems that you're giving your best to find new recruits."

"Lord Mask?!" Sisbell's voice cracked. "Wh-why are you here...?"

CHAPTER 4

"Just on a holiday. I wanted to forget all about what's happening in the country. There shouldn't be anything strange about that." The masked man dramatically shook his head.

Iska wordlessly backed away. He had seen this man before. This was not a man who was easy to deal with.

...This is the guy who restrained Captain Mismis! ...This is an independent state—not the Sovereignty or a battlefield. Why is he here?

Iska had fought against Kissing the purebred, but he had remembered the uncanniness of this man, who commanded her and whose nature he didn't know.

"You're the one who's strange, Sisbell." He pointed at her.

She started to tremble.

"I wonder who this boy standing next to you could be."

"This…is…"

"There's no need to lie. I encountered this Imperial swordsman during the incident with the vortex. Though we were both unsatisfied with the outcome. Heh-heh," he chuckled from beneath his mask.

"Luck is on my side. I never would have known he was an Imperial soldier if I hadn't been involved with the incident in Mudor Canyon. And it is already too late. I have proof of your conversation."

The masked man made a show of holding a recorder out in front of him before tucking it away in the breast pocket of his suit.

"This will devastate the queen. To think her own daughter had ties to the Empire."

"Wait, Lord Mask! I'm not colluding with the enemy. If anything, it is the opposite. I'm trying to save the country from traitors by—"

"You're the traitor," he calmly interrupted.

"…Ugh." She gaped at him. "I see what you're trying to do…"

Her voice was cold. With wild rage in her eyes that was unfamiliar to Iska, the girl glared at the masked man and his subordinates.

"To the Zoa family, the truth is not important. You want fragments of the conversation that you can spin to support your narrative. Your goal is to deceive the queen."

"You are free to think what you like. It's already too late."

"...Who told you where I would be?"

"I will say this again, but I was just visiting the resort. Unfortunately for you, Sisbell, I must take you in on suspicions of consorting with the enemy."

All four of his subordinates stood ready at once.

Before Iska could say anything, the blond girl turned her back on them, sprinting for her life into the oil extraction facility along the dim night road.

"You're running? I should have expected that from the queen's daughter. I thought you would obediently let yourself be captured, but it seems you plan to struggle to the end. Chasing you in the darkness of night will be a task."

"...So you're Lord Mask."

Chasing after Sisbell from the corner of his eye, Iska turned to face the man.

"Aren't you supposed to be in this together? You're both part of the royal palace, right?"

"If you're asking about our relationship, then there is only one answer: *Yeah, right.*"

Stifled resentment flooded out of the mask.

"The Sovereignty is not a monolith. You must have experienced that firsthand. That girl schemed to make an Imperial soldier into her underling, of all things. That is a serious crime."

"...You don't want to know why she reached out to me?"

Princess Sisbell had confided in Iska that she had no allies.

CHAPTER 4

Though he couldn't accept her proposal because of his position, even Iska had seen his decision had left her in distress. The girl was risking her own life to protect the country.

...She's just like Alice... We're enemies and incompatible with each other, but I understand where she's coming from.

"Isn't she part of the royal family? Don't you feel like there's something up if she has a reason to ask for help from an Imperial soldier?"

"I'm sick of this conversation." Lord Mask sighed. "I don't care about her reasons. We're talking about the fight for the throne. She committed treason. She tried to bring in an Imperial soldier to the fight. There is no reason for me to ask why she cheated. Breaking the rules is a crime."

"In that case—"

"Making a commotion in the middle of the night is a crime, too. Don't make me file a noise complaint."

An intense ray of light shone in on them. One of the facility lamps had been turned on and lit the grounds as brightly as midday.

"Jhin?!"

"Jeez. I heard you were running late, and I was wondering what you were up to. I can't believe you've gotten yourself mixed up with the wrong crowd. See, boss? This isn't the right time to take our time choosing a barbecue place."

"Did you really have to bring that up now?!"

Jhin and Captain Mismis had appeared from the shadows of the extractor machine. Nene jumped out after them, carefully clutching Iska's astral swords.

"Uh, it's that guy from back then... He's the sorcerer who kicked me!"

"If it isn't my dear hostage. I thought I'd pushed you into the vortex, but it seems you've made it back alive. Wonderful. I believe you've been in good health?"

The two had a deep connection. Singled out by Mismis, Lord Mask shrugged as though he was amused.

"Hmm, I see. In other words, Sisbell wasn't just seeking a single pawn. She was trying to recruit an entire unit."

"Stop spouting nonsense."

The silver-haired sniper set his eyes on the four grunts, who did not so much as tremble. The man Sisbell had called "Lord Mask" had to be a purebred. In that case, that made them his accompanying guards.

"Don't get the wrong idea," warned Lord Mask. "Though you seek a battle, we do not."

"...What was that?"

"We came here to retrieve our kindred. We have no desire to play with fire in Alsamira."

He had the conversation between Princess Sisbell and an Imperial swordsman recorded on a device, though they didn't know what Lord Mask aimed to use it for.

...What should I do? I need to make a call right here.

...We don't have a reason to fight for Sisbell as her shields.

That applied to Captain Mismis, Jhin, and Nene in particular.

Lord Mask could scheme all he wanted. This was an internal conflict of interest within an enemy nation. It required no intervention from the Imperial unit.

"Looks like you got the picture. Let's focus on capturing Princess Sisbell. Make sure you play nice. Though she is a traitor, it would be annoying if we had to face public backlash for injuring a princess."

The masked man snapped his fingers. The ones who answered his call were *not* the four men behind him—but something entirely *outside* their expectations.

CHAPTER 4

Iska and the rest of Unit 907 and even the elites of the Nebulis Sovereignty who Lord Mask led were taken aback by the intruder's abrupt entry.

"...What *is* that?"

Pushing past mounds of desert sand, a gigantic object dropped from the sky, tearing through the curtain of night.

The thing had crashed onto the ground, making the earth rumble.

...It was a heavily armored machine, pitch-black.

The giant was shaped like a human, one that had built muscle on top of muscle. It had to be about ten feet tall, covered in multiple layers of armored plates. It hummed with the energy of a large truck.

It held an enormous, reinforced sword in its right hand. Its left hand sported a riot shield. It looked almost exactly like a knight. Its grave appearance even made Lord Mask leap back out of caution.

"Is that an Object? One of the extermination machines?!" Nene yelled through the dust cloud.

"No way... I've never heard of one of these being deployed outside the Empire."

"Astral energy detected," announced a mechanical voice.

Its large frame swiveled, looking at the people gathered at the oil drilling facility, appraising them. Its gaze landed on Lord Mask and his subordinates.

"Astral power in one, two, three, four, five..."

Finally, the machine turned to Mismis.

"Six. Tally complete. Initiating pursuit of target 'Purebred 9LC' for prioritized restraint."

"...*No!*" Nene's shriek was in vain.

The armored machine leaped high into the air, making a beeline for the interior of the oil drilling facility. It was headed toward where Princess Sisbell had run to hide.

"Iska, we need to go after that machine! We can't let it get away! We need to destroy it!" Nene yelled.

"But isn't that an Imperial weapon?"

...The Object. I'm pretty sure that was the name of the unmanned robot display model... An anti–astral power weapon.

It was supposed to be their ally. As a top-class engineer, Nene would know the most about it. Then why was she acting this way?

"It got data on *the captain*."

"...I see!"

"What? Uh. D-did I do something wrong?" Mismis asked.

"You can keep quiet and feign ignorance, boss. Iska and Nene, go after that huge thing!" yelled Jhin, piercing through the night.

Propelled by his energy, Iska and Nene didn't miss a beat as they both launched off the ground at the same time.

...The robot counted Captain Mismis as the sixth member with astral power... If it gets back to the Empire, then we're over. Headquarters will know the captain turned into a witch!

That was why they needed to stop it.

"What's going on? You're destroying it? ...Are you planning on *pinning the blame on us*?!" Lord Mask barked in a cold rage. He must have realized what the Imperial unit was scheming. "You four! Capture Princess Sisbell and evacuate!"

"We're not going to let you do that."

A gunshot pierced through the darkness. A bullet tore through the air right in front of the eyes of the astral mages as they were about to start their pursuit.

"Hurry up and go. Nene, don't lag behind."

"Leave it to me!"

CHAPTER 4

Nene sped up. She was right behind Iska. They could still make it in time. They followed the Object going after Sisbell.

The dust started to settle.

The two Imperial soldiers and five astral mages remained in the hushed area.

"You're getting on my nerves." The man tapped the front of his mask with an extended finger. "We had no intention of escalating things. Our goal was to take home one of our fellow mages. Why would an Imperial soldier protect her?"

"You've got the wrong idea."

"Hmm?"

"You're clever, but you only think in circles."

The silver-haired sniper moved forward in place of Mismis. Lord Mask hadn't noticed the silent rage in the calm voice of the Imperial soldier.

"It was you—the one who dropped the boss into the vortex," Jhin said.

"..."

"There's your reason."

Though only the two of them would be challenging the five elites, including a purebred, Jhin did not have second thoughts about his will to fight or his self-confidence.

"That's why I want to give you a good beating."

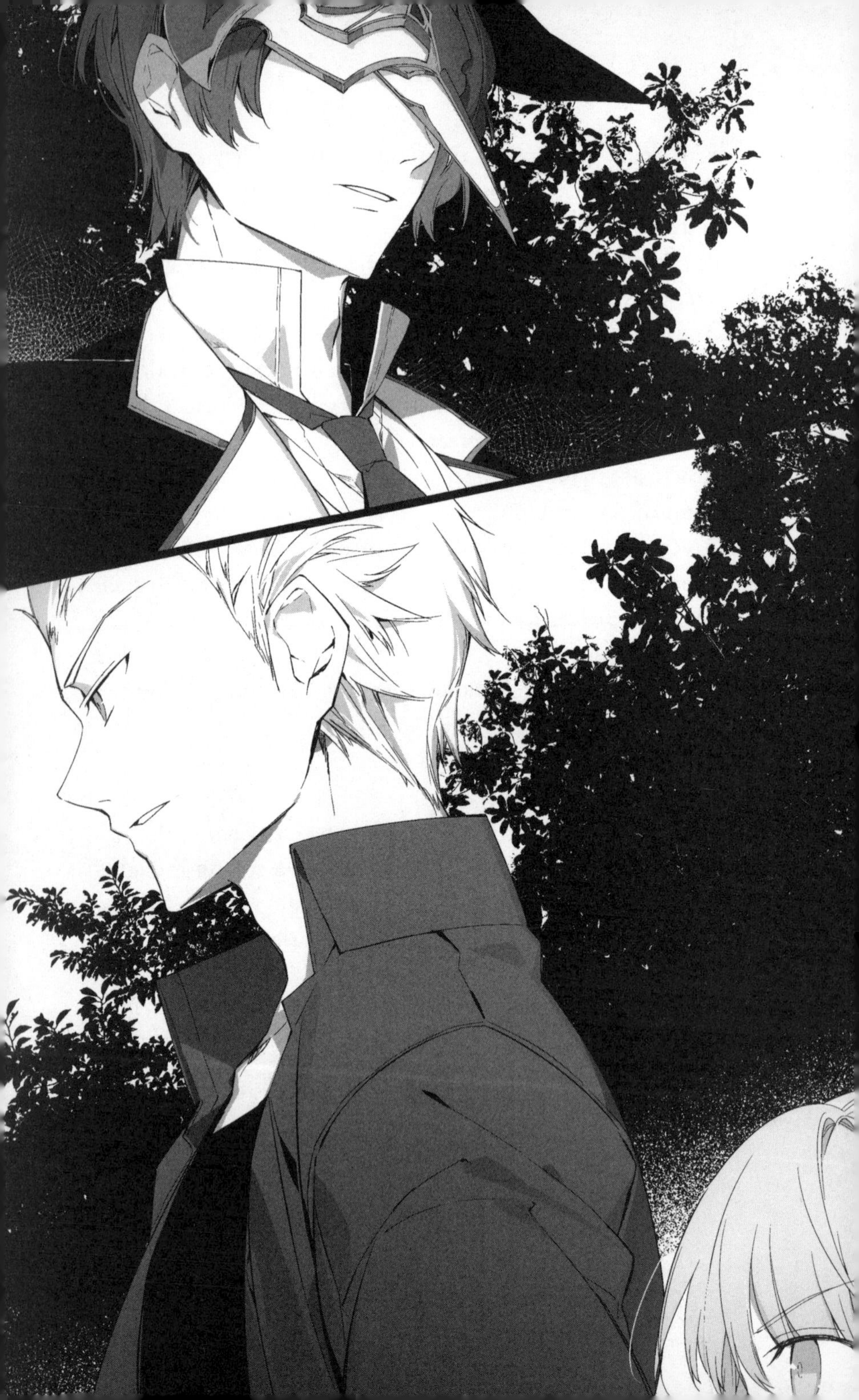

CHAPTER 4

When the Object was in flight, it emitted a white trail of light and vapor in the air.

...The Object is a generic model name... I know that it's supposed to be a witch-hunting machinated soldier made by the Imperial research institute.

It was an executioner—one that would detect astral energy and pursue witches. The main issue of concern was the way this one operated.

They didn't know whether it was the mass-produced variety from the Omen Institute for Astral Research or a custom-made model from the first generation. It could have been an "unofficial" model that hadn't been announced to the public.

"But they don't have parts that allow them to fly. I haven't even heard of something that can make the propulsion required for this big machine to fly through the air," Nene said.

"...So it's a newer model?"

"I'm not sure. I think that it's a model of the Object, though."

They headed to where the trail of light continued.

Iska kept running through the facility grounds with Nene. The trail of light was slowly making a descent. It had probably found its target.

Sisbell the Witch.

"Anyway, Iska, we can't let that robot get back to the capital!" Nene shouted between pants. "Captain Mismis was counted as a witch. If headquarters sees that data, they'll find out that the captain has astral power!"

"I know that. We can stop that happening by destroying it, right?"

But they couldn't *just* destroy it. The Object was after the purebred Sisbell. Headquarters would see this as an attempt by Sisbell and her guards.

...In the end, it'll mean I need to save Sisbell... But this is going to be the last time!

He couldn't extend his hand to a princess of an enemy country...because the descendants of the Founder were the very people Iska needed to capture to realize his wish for peace.

"Are you trying to say that you desire peace? That's impossible."

"That's why I thought about catching a direct descendant from Nebulis's bloodline."

In the history of the century-long war, the Imperial Army had never once captured a purebred.

That was what he had been told. Iska believed it. That was exactly why *he* needed to be the one to do it.

And he never would have guessed...

"My name is Sisbell. I am honored you remember me.

"I am Sisbell Lou Nebulis IX, a candidate to be the next queen."

How had this happened? What an inexplicable turn of fate. He never would have guessed that he had let a purebred he was meant to capture escape with his very own hands.

...And it's the same now... When she's right in front of me, I'm choosing to save her instead of capturing her.

He was saving Captain Mismis. He was going to destroy the Object.

He didn't have the time to restrain a purebred.

"This has got me beat..." He couldn't help but bark in

laughter, even during this serious scene. "I was sure I was putting everything on the line, but things have gone off the rails. An ironic twist of fate."

"Iska?"

"...Let's hurry, Nene. We can't let the Object get away."

He gritted his back teeth as he catapulted off the ground and pursued the trail of light.

5

NO TRESPASSING.

She jumped over a handrail with the sign. Looking up at the towering oil drills, she went deeper and deeper into the grounds. Sisbell ran without a destination in mind.

"...Uh...ha...ah...!"

Where was she headed?

She was out of breath and sweating.

But where would she hide?

She knew she would be captured. Even if she waited through the night, concealing herself in the shadow of the oil drills, Lord Mask's subordinates would find her in the morning.

Even if she ran to the Sovereignty without being caught, her conversation with an Imperial soldier had been recorded.

There was no point to it anymore.

She'd be damned if she did and damned if she didn't.

"Uh...ha, ah...uh...guh!"

This was the end.

She would be imprisoned as a traitor. That meant anyone who could have battled against "that monster" in the royal family would be gone. They would go after her mother's life. Their government would be destroyed, and the Nebulis Sovereignty would be led to ruin.

They would be heading toward all-out war against the Empire. They would continue battling until this planet was destroyed and then, finally, no one would be left.

Why am I still running...?

Her vision was blurring from the tears building up in her eyes.

Her heels weren't suited to running. They were close to falling right off her feet. She was wheezing. Her sides had started to hurt.

But then why?

"...Don't you dare underestimate me!"

She was obstinate.

Even if she was blamed for a crime when she was innocent, even if they tried to confine her, Princess Sisbell still had a job to do...*to figure out who the traitor was.*

"Lord Mask! Who told you about me?!"

Sisbell never officially announced where she would be going. Even within the palace, only a small handful of people knew this classified information. Her keeper, Shuvalts, had been by her side, where he could keep an eye on her. Her mother was out of the question. Because of that, the only suspects were her older sisters, Elletear and Aliceliese. It must have been one of them.

...If I can just get back to the palace, I can check with Illumination...and find out who contacted Lord Mask.

Even if she had to crawl through the desert, she would survive out of pure spite and get back to the palace. She could be captured *after* that. If she could just tell her mother, she might be able to protect the queen's life...which meant the Sovereignty by extension.

CHAPTER 4

"Protecting the country...is the duty of a princess!"

She would not yield.

She could be stubborn. Even if her mother and the retainers found her suspicious, until she completely fulfilled her responsibilities as a princess—

"Prioritized target for restraint: 'Purebred 9LC' has been secured."

...

...Huh?

"Purebred 9LC." Sisbell realized that it meant her. A cold, mechanical voice and a gigantic shadow dropped down from the sky...right before her eyes.

"An Object?! A mechanized Imperial soldier... I hope they didn't...pass along my information to the Empire!"

It wasn't just Lord Mask. The traitor had even told the Empire that Sisbell would be visiting this country.

"Gah!"

She didn't hesitate for a moment to change course. She turned her back on the machine that stood in her way and ran for it.

"Skree."

She heard an unpleasant sound. There was something creaking between her feet. Immediately, Sisbell's right leg lost mobility. A sharp pain ran through her body from her left calf, making her lower body convulse.

"Suppression bullet fired."

She tumbled over from the impact. She couldn't do anything as she hit the hard ground. She prepared herself—

"Right in the nick of time."

What? Sisbell had just been about to collide with the ground. But now she was being held up by someone.

"Iska, it's shifted into auto-elimination mode. Be careful!"

"I know."

The Imperial swordsman prepared his black and white swords. He positioned himself as though to shield Sisbell, who was immediately behind him.

"I guess I can't say I'm only doing this once. This is the second time, after all."

The former Saint Disciple Iska.

The swordsman who had broken her out of prison one year ago turned around with a complicated smile on his face.

"I wonder why our fates are so connected."

CHAPTER 5

Execution by Witch Hunter

1

In the shopping streets of Alsamira, the shadows of night deepened, and blowing through the gaps of buildings was a wind cold enough to chill anyone to their core.

"This is bad. It's gotten so late."

While dragging along a travel cart, Alice wound her way through the silent main roads with long strides. She had crossed the sprawling desert and the suburbs lined with luxury homes in a taxi. A few moments ago, she had arrived at the shopping street.

...Rin looked up the hotel where Sisbell was staying.

...But I guess it's dinnertime? Or she might already be sleeping by now.

She had been hoping to invite her sister out to dinner. But because they had found those eerie tracks crossing the desert, the bus had unsurprisingly been delayed.

They were footprints, traces of something much larger than a human lurking in the desert.

*　　＊　　＊*

Whatever had passed through must have been much larger than any human. Based on the traces of machine oil, Alice had deduced the culprit was likely one of the mechanized soldiers from the Empire. That was why she had been quick to run toward them.

"I thought the Empire had sent it over, intending to invade this country...but that doesn't feel right."

The outskirts of town and the streets were quiet. If even a single machinated soldier had stepped foot in those places, the guards would have been making a scene.

"...Lady Alice?"

"What?"

She heard a voice from right in front of her. It was almost as though her eyes hadn't even registered the senior who had walked up. Her head had been occupied with thoughts about the nature of the footprints and hypothetical conversations with her sister.

"I knew it! It *is* you, Lady Alice!"

It was the older gentleman wearing a perfect suit. It was the keeper Shuvalts. He had been Sisbell's attendant since her youth—the one and only servant who had known what was on Sisbell's mind since she began sequestering herself in her room.

"Shuvalts. What a coincidence..."

She was suddenly flustered on the inside.

If this man was in the shopping district, that meant that Sisbell had to be somewhere nearby. *Oh no! I'm not prepared! I never imagined I would accidentally bump into them so soon.*

"Uh, is Sisbell—?"

"Have you seen Lady Sisbell?!"

"...Excuse me?"

What did that mean?

Had her sister been separated from her keeper?

CHAPTER 5

"I haven't been able to get into contact with her. She told me she had several matters she needed to attend to alone."

"What?"

I need details. Now. Under the streetlamps, Alice took a step toward the older man—

Fwoosht, a bluish light zipped through the empty sky.

"Huh?!"

It came from the outskirts of town, far from the shopping district. It was where Alice had been.

…It's far away, even farther than the vacation homes in the residential areas… Could that be coming from above the oil drilling facility?

The light melted into the black of night instantly, but if she could see it on the ground from this distance, it must have been blinding.

Alice thought it looked similar to the telltale light of astral energy.

"Lady Alice, what's wrong?"

The older man looked at Alice, seemingly not noticing the light behind him. She was sure there were no other people who had witnessed it from the streets or the hotel windows.

"It can't be. But it can't be anyone besides the Imperial Army!"

The footprints in the desert came back to her mind. She doubted that the Imperial Army would openly attack this country, but Alice currently knew the Empire had plenty of motives.

There was a purebred witch here—Sisbell. The Imperial Army would have no reservations when it came to the daughter of the Sovereignty's queen.

…But why would they know Sisbell's location? …Very few know that she's away.

That included Alice, the queen, and their oldest sister, Elletear.

The Zoa and Hydra Houses had their own intelligence networks, which meant they might have had some intel. But that should have been all.

Had someone sold Sisbell out to the Empire?

"You need to think about that later, Alice," she said to herself. "There's a chance that there are Imperial soldiers sneaking around. If that light was part of a battle..."

"Lady Alice?"

"Shuvalts, I'll leave my things with you. Please wait for orders here until you hear back from Sisbell!"

She abandoned the cart and ran into the night, heading toward the outskirts—to the oil drilling facility that bordered the desert.

"The Imperial Army chose the wrong person to cross."

She cut through the freezing wind. She didn't care that they were estranged. Sisbell was weak. Her sister couldn't protect herself all alone.

In that case...she had an obligation to protect her younger sister.

"I won't forgive anyone who puts a hand on Sisbell!"

2

Astral power research was the one field of study forbidden within the Empire, but there was an exception: the single accumulation of intellect called "Omen."

It was an astral power research institute that had been established through a vote by the Eight Great Apostles. One of the things that had come out of that institute was the Object. The Witch Hunter. The executioner and soldier.

CHAPTER 5

And it was in front of her very eyes.

"...Wh-what is this, Iska?" Sisbell looked up in fear. "Why is it chasing after me? You weren't the one...who suggested that they send this weapon after all this time, were you?"

"I don't have that kind of authority. I stopped being a Saint Disciple a year ago."

"..."

Sisbell must have understood that. Iska had lost his position as a Saint Disciple. That had been his punishment after breaking her out of prison.

"In that case..." The princess bit her lip. "Why are you doing this now? Didn't you say that you wouldn't be my ally?"

"Yeah, you're right."

"Then why are you here and—?"

"It was the same a year ago."

"What?"

"It was the same a year ago. I'm an Imperial soldier, and you're a Sovereign mage. I can't be your ally, but I helped you out anyway. I haven't changed since then."

"..."

"I have my reasons, too... I have a whole mountain of things I haven't told you about."

Iska carried the pair of astral swords—one white and the other black—that he had inherited from his master in the past and turned to face the "mobile weapon."

"Restraint target 'Purebred 9LC.'"

This weapon could distinguish only between "enemies" and "non-enemies." Anyone who interfered with it restraining a witch was considered the former. That was because an Imperial soldier saving a witch was unthinkable. It had been programmed to think that way.

"We're going to destroy this thing. My friends are stopping that masked guy from chasing after you."

The ones who had destroyed the Object were Sovereign astral mages. Things could get messy if Lord Mask made his appearance if Iska was trying to deceive headquarters.

"…You're going to help me?"

"Short answer, yes. At least, we're not planning on handing you off to the Object or Lord Mask."

"Nh!"

The petite princess turned her face down. She still had a lot more growing to do compared to her sister Alice.

"…Iska," she said in her youthful voice. "You're so unfair. You're always leading me on…and it makes me want to depend on you…"

"That is a separate conversation."

The mechanized soldier began to rev. After a beat, Iska launched off the ground. The Object waved the reinforced ceramic long sword from its steel arm that protruded from its back.

"Nene, let's go with the usual plan."

"Leave it to me!"

He ran straight at the Object from the front on his own.

…It's gone into auto-elimination mode…and is treating me as an enemy already.

He was the witch's ally. In other words, he was the Empire's enemy.

A blade of wind roared through the space.

The machinated soldier had adapted to the deep night by its jet-black exterior, and even the arm that gripped its sword was gray. It was difficult to see the blade, but Iska took his best aim and brought down his black astral sword.

CHAPTER 5

"Ha!"

"—"

They were the only pair of astral swords in the world.

His opponent was wielding a ceramic long sword that had been reinforced with refined crystal through techniques developed in the Empire. Both blades could cut through steel, crossing each other.

And then they bounced off each other.

"...Gah?"

The ear-piercing grating of metals echoed, and Iska felt himself flying through the air. On impact, he was sent toward the fence that surrounded the oil drilling equipment.

"Whoa, Iska?!"

"Iska!"

Nene and Sisbell shouted.

Like a cat, he flipped through the air and barely managed to land on his two feet as he approached the fence from behind.

...It's like a tiger against a mouse... I knew that going into this, but it's not a match for a human.

The mass of steel must have neared a weight of eleven tons, driven by kinetic energy. If he could only use physical strength, he would be unilaterally outdone.

"I hate that I can't tell what it's thinking..."

It didn't have a moment of buildup before it moved like a human. And because its steel arm was attached to its back, its movements were incredibly difficult to capture. It was fundamentally different from a human swordsman.

"I'll try again—"

He put the white sword away in its sheath. If his opponent wasn't an astral mage, this wasn't the time to use the white blade. He let his free left hand join his right hand and supported the black blade with a two-handed grip.

"This is it."

He avoided the reinforced ceramic long sword and circled around to the side of the Object. Before its gigantic revolving form could follow him, Iska aimed for its steel legs and brought down his sword.

CRUNCH.

The astral blade had been stopped…by the other hand that came from the Object's back—by the wall created by the riot shield.

"…This isn't any normal shield."

The shield had been created as a countermeasure against witches and sorcerers, made with the goal of defending against fire, water, and lightning types of astral power. On the other hand, it lacked strength. All it could do was just about stop a bullet from a handgun.

"One cut, huh."

He had left a light dent with his sword on the thick shield. How many times would it take until the shield broke?

"Iska! Wh-what's giving you so much trouble?!" Sisbell was shouting from where she was withdrawn near the fence. "You call yourself a Saint Disciple? Don't you have…a stronger skill? Like a secret trick! An ace up your sleeve! Something! Anything?!"

"A secret what?"

"S-something!"

"Nope."

"Excuse me?!"

"I specialize in anti–astral mage stuff."

That was because he had been *trained* that way under the instruction of the strongest swordsman in the Empire. If he was facing an astral mage, he would have been able to even keep up with one of the Founder's descendants.

On the other hand, when it came to hand-to-hand combat, he

was perfectly mediocre, if Iska was to fight other Saint Disciples. Getting to the top was almost unattainable for him. That was his destiny because Iska was a swordsman. He had astral swords that specialized in fighting astral attacks.

"Wh-what?! You only specialize in astral mages...?"

"You heard me."

...Even if I haven't fought in front of Sisbell before...hasn't she at least heard about me from Alice?

When he thought about it, Kissing had also not known about Iska's swords. He had thought that the royal family connected by the Founder's blood would have all shared the knowledge of his swords' secrets.

"To be honest, I'm not really compatible with this kind of opponent. I can't fight large things."

"...Th-then what are we going to do?!" Sisbell shrieked.

"Nene!" Iska jumped away from the ceramic long sword that came down on him. "How many more seconds?"

"I think I'm ready to go. I've finished transmitting our coordinates!" yelled back the girl with the ponytail. "I did it really fast, but I think that the trajectory is correct!"

She raised her palm directly into the air, holding up a mechanism in the shape of a ring on her pinkie finger. Did the witch notice it was flashing?

"Satellite 'the Star of Tetrabiblos.' A piercing shot!"

When Nene yelled out her instructions, there was a huge explosion, and the Object's riot shield was blown to smithereens. There had been a shell dropping down from a high altitude, released from high in the sky above the clouds. It had hit the shield with accurate aim.

"What? ...Huh? ...Wh-what was that just now?!" Sisbell's eyes opened wide.

What in the world had happened? They were right in the middle of the desert. Where had the shell come flying from? She hadn't seen a tank nearby with ammunition.

It had all been made possible with the satellite weapon, the Star of Tetrabiblos. The Department of Suppression Weapons Development had launched it into the sky in the past and left it in Nene's care.

It was like a pet that was attached by the hip to its owner. This satellite weapon moved through the sky, adjusting its location according to Nene's position.

"The one in charge of our unit's firepower isn't me... It's Nene."

"And again!" Nene cried.

Another shot broke the ceramic long sword into pieces, making its way through the armor. She had wanted a piercing shot. The shells were hard and heavy. When they could accelerate during a free fall from high up in the air, they had been able to break the Object's sword and shield.

"We've got one left, Iska!"

"Got it."

With the next shot, they would break through the Object's armor, and Iska would destroy the exposed machinery that drove it.

Psht. He heard air whooshing out of something.

The imposing sound echoed, and the armor covering the Object burst open.

"We did it! We broke through the armor! Okay, Iska, hurry and get the machine—" prompted Sisbell.

"..."

"Iska?"

"That's not what happened," Nene answered. "I haven't ordered the third one. That wasn't my ammunition just now."

CHAPTER 5

"Wh-what does that mean…?"

"*Rejecting…armor detachment.*"

It was as though the Object were shedding its skin. One and then two of the outermost layers on the gigantic machine peeled off and dropped to the ground.

…Why is it taking off its own armor? …I've never seen anything move this fast in automatic mode before, Iska thought.

Nene hadn't, either. She tried determining what had happened to the machine before her eyes and gulped.

"*Suspend primary energy supply. Converting to secondary source.*"

The Witch Hunter started to transform after its sword and shield had been destroyed, abandoning the armor that protected it.

"Wh-what is this machine?! Iska?!"

"…This is my first time seeing an Object like this."

It was like a bipedal mechanical beast. After peeling off its armor, all that was left was a wide-open hollow like a beast's maw. Iska saw an eerie blue spark coming to life inside it.

"What is that…?"

The glow was released from the entire machine, gathered at the center of the gigantic mouth. The oil drilling facilities in the night lit everything up as though it was midday.

"What is this…? Iska, there's something wrong with that light. It's too strong!" Nene yelled. She narrowed her eyes against the blinding light. "This isn't electricity. It's not fuel. What…? What could be the source of this power…?"

"It's the light from *astral energy*!" Sisbell exclaimed.

Shiver.

Iska ran as fast as he could to Nene.

"Get down, Nene!"

When he grabbed on to the girl with the ponytail, he threw himself down onto the hard ground.

"Life-form integra—cannon for planetary disassembly."

It was "something" that had been turned into a flash. The belt of light made a high-pitched sound, blowing through the space that Iska and Nene had been standing in and heading to the oil drilling equipment behind them.

It burned through the fence and cut through a gigantic steel crane like butter, melting it in half. It burned through the empty air.

The flame that burned through the heavens, scorching the drilling area.

When the hellfire and sparks blazed, it turned into a disastrous scene, as though the blaze at the prison spire in Alcatroz were being revived.

…Was that just one shot? …That single flash made a mass of steel melt and already started fires.

This was no laughing matter. If this were brought out onto the battlefield, the Imperial soldiers and everything else would get caught up in the blast, ally or not, and result in total destruction.

"Iska."

Nene's face was pale, illuminated by the embers. She was pointing at the Object, slender now that it had shed its outer armor.

"There has definitely got to be something in the machinery in there."

"…Yeah."

He gripped his astral swords. He didn't know whether the cold sweat on his forehead came from the blaze itself.

"Object! Your light…" Then he yelled, *"What are you hiding inside you?"*

CHAPTER 5

In the oil drilling facility, near its entrance, two Imperial soldiers were lit by the illumination of the streetlamps as they ran past the front of the prefabricated warehouses.

"Jh-Jhin, this is bad! They're coming after us!"

"Boss, hurry up and get over here!"

The petite captain looked desperate as she ran over the asphalt road, and the silver-haired sniper sprinted by her side.

They dove behind the warehouses.

The bright lights of the oil drilling machinery didn't reach that far. If they kept themselves hidden, even wild beasts wouldn't have been able to find them.

"L-looks like they haven't found us…"

"Don't stick your face out. We still don't know what kind of astral powers they can weaponize."

If they had scouting or searching abilities, then they could have even sensed the body heat where they were hidden. At the moment, all they could do was pray that their opponents couldn't do that.

"The Empire is only aware of a handful of astral powers, and even if two people are fire types, they can use them in an infinite number of ways. There's no such thing as too much caution."

"…Y-yeah," Mismis answered hesitantly, intently looking at Jhin's right arm in the darkness. She was staring at his torn battle uniform. The fabric at his right elbow had been ripped, and there was some faint red welt on his exposed arm.

"Um, uh, sorry… I didn't notice…"

"There's nothing we can do about it. I would have still gotten hit if I was in your position. Besides, it was my fault. Iska warned me."

Be careful of the masked man.

He could interfere with space and time, which was an incredibly rare ability. He seemed to be able to move as though he were leaping through space, going around to the back of his targets—without making a sound.

"What was that again about 'tying things up neatly right here'? That fraud." He spoke calmly.

The masked man had tried to stab Mismis in the back. Right as the man had teleported behind her and tried to kill her, Jhin barely managed to fire his gun and fend him off.

"The Imperial assassin's unit was freaked out, too. This guy's not a sorcerer—he's an assassin."

Jhin had doubted his eyes when he saw Iska's wounded back after the battle over the vortex.

To think Iska had been taken from the back. That was the former Saint Disciple they were talking about.

He wondered how many masters would be able to do that if he searched through the entire Empire. His doubt was finally undone now.

"...I—I wonder if he's a purebred?"

"Most likely. I don't think the world would last long if tons of people like him were around."

He tore the cloth around his cut and exposed more of his wound.

He held his arm and applied pressure on it until he started to bleed. He was making preparations in case the knife had been tainted with poison, trying to take drastic measures by squeezing out the poison along with his blood.

"But we haven't got any problems. Iska and Nene will destroy the Object. We'll pretend they did it and evacuate."

Their opponents were five mages, including a purebred.

They only had two people. Trying to fight would come with huge risks. The two of them hadn't come to fight. They were still in the middle of their extended vacation. If they could just buy some time, that was enough.

Though, to be honest, Jhin wanted to catch them off guard...

"Boss, have you seen that blond girl Iska was talking to before?"

"Oh! I guess that bothered you, too. I haven't seen her before, either."

She had been facing Iska. Before they could get close enough to listen to the conversation, the blond girl had turned her back on Iska and started running.

"It looked to me like the Object went flying after her."

"Th-then is she a witch?!"

"Plus, the masked guy said something like, *We're taking our kindred and going home.* In other words, he was after the blond chick."

He leaned out of the warehouse slightly. After checking several times that he couldn't see anyone on the road, Jhin sighed.

"But this is what gets me. I wonder if she's a big deal?"

"Huh? Wh-who?"

"I know she's a witch, but she's just a little girl. And there are five full-grown adults trying to take her home, including that purebred masked guy."

"Oh?! I—I see!"

"She must be important. They don't seem like they're 'taking her home.' With the force they're using, it looks like they're 'dragging her back.' I think..."

"Looks like you've teased out the details with a little game of detective."

The voice came from above them, but when Jhin and Mismis looked up, all they could see was faint light from the stars.

"A snake in the grass. I think it best you don't stick your head into this if you don't want to get hurt."

It was coming from the roof of the warehouse. With the light behind him, the masked man was staring right down at them.

"We'll shut you up."

"Jump!" Jhin pushed the captain's back as he leaped out from the shadow of the warehouse.

Sparks flared up. Before they could blink, the warehouse was enveloped in flames. It seemed to have caught fire using astral magic.

"Are you out of your minds...?!" Mismis hollered with disheveled blue hair. "This isn't a battlefield! This is an establishment in either the Empire or the Sovereignty...!"

"Don't worry about it."

The masked man jumped down from the burning warehouse, leaping from a height of three stories. But the only impact from his pliable fall was taken by the tips of his shoes.

"You will be the ones wanted for destroying personal property. We were the ones who stopped you when you went on a rampage. You won't even need to stand witness."

The losers would shoulder all blame for the crimes. He had flipped their attempt to put the blame of the Object's destruction onto the Sovereignty.

"You have nothing to worry about. Just relax."

White fog began to gather. They doubted it was a naturally occurring phenomenon in the desert. The mist approached Jhin and Mismis with unusual speed, as though it were trying to engulf them.

"*Again?* Boss, over here!"

Jhin launched off the ground, clucking his tongue and jumping away from the fog. This mist had been created through astral power. But that itself couldn't hurt them. The dangerous part was that it could blind people from other astral attacks.

CHAPTER 5

...*Splish*. They heard the sound of dripping water from immediately behind them.

"Jhin, *it's coming from behind us!*"

"I know."

The green liquid was stealthily slithering toward his shoes. The liquid was filled with bumpy bubbles. Some kind of paralyzing poison. If their ankles were submerged in it, they would be rendered immobilized. If it got onto his arms, he wouldn't be able to hold his gun.

"This is getting annoying." Jhin clucked his tongue.

The sniper's normal abilities were considerably restrained in the melee.

After reading the terrain and the direction of the wind...and in just a few seconds, he could even see the movements of the enemy, right down to the trajectory of their fired shots. With inhuman focus, he would hone his senses and shoot at the most important actors in the enemy group. The front guard would support him. If Iska had been there, he would have taken all the fire from the five mages and made an "opening" for Jhin to shoot Lord Mask.

The sniper didn't have a solid grip on time or space.

"I can be a decoy...," Mismis offered.

"Not a chance. You can't just do stuff like you did in the prison spire. Think about how you can fight with the hand you've been dealt."

He held his sniper rifle and rolled along the ground. He didn't even have time to look through the scope. He attempted a split-second feat to aim at Lord Mask.

"Oh? You seem to be an acrobat, sniper."

"Don't move. I don't like wasting bullets."

"As you wish."

The masked man's form wavered and disappeared. After a

moment, Jhin heard the sound of a quiet footstep immediately behind him.

"You need not worry. I'll end things before you even need to fire your precious bullets."

"You're right." He wrenched his body around as fast as he could.

...*This is the third time. I knew the sorcerer would definitely aim for my back.*

He stopped the knife that the masked man had brought up. The moment that Jhin saw the knife's blade glitter in the night at the edge of his vision, it disappeared from in front of him.

"You thought I could only teleport myself?"

The knife had gone from the man's right hand to his left, transporting through space. Jhin's right hand had been trying to grab the knife, but it cut through the empty air. Instead, he was stabbed deeply by the blade.

"Jhin?!" Mismis yelled.

"Looks like you can't carry your sniper gun anymore."

"I don't need it."

He brought up his left hand. The silver-haired sniper was carrying an automatic pistol hidden in the palm of his hand. Though it didn't have dependable firepower, at this distance, he wasn't scared of missing.

"No!"

"I told you. You're pretty clever, but you're prone to thinking in circles."

Jhin would have predicted the man would go around to his back. Even if he brought a knife down on the sniper, Jhin would have dodged a fatal wound. In that case, he would have aimed for the sniper's right arm, which carried his gun. If he could no longer use his weapon, he was nothing to fear.

Jhin had perfectly predicted Lord Mask's ideas in a split second.

CHAPTER 5

"You knew what I was after—"

"Of course."

He couldn't teleport fast enough.

The gun fired.

The gunpowder exploded out of Jhin's gun. It hit. He had no way of protecting himself. Even Lord Mask had readied himself in that moment.

But the bullet stopped.

Metal scraped against something. Something on the other side of the black suit that Lord Mask wore, under the fabric, had stopped the bullet.

"...What?!"

"How unfortunate for you, Imperial soldier. Well, I was surprised by your cleverness."

A hole had opened in the chest of his black clothes.

Peeking out from the hole was a tiny, broken device that had stopped the bullet. It was *the recording device that had documented Iska and Sisbell's conversation.*

In exchange for losing his proof that would condemn Sisbell, the masked sorcerer had won.

"The planet has smiled favorably upon me!" He punched away Jhin's handgun.

"Stop!"

"Too late."

As the masked man calmly walked away, he kicked Mismis to the ground as she tried to run to them. He was staggering slightly from the impact of getting shot in the chest.

"I wouldn't want to catch fire after finding out you have a grenade or something else hidden away. I will be making my escape."

"...What...did you say?" Jhin wiped at his split lip with his hand. "What was that about catching fire?"

"We've found it. Before we could think of checking on your hiding place in the warehouse, we searched the grounds. And then we found this."

A gigantic barrel rolled down the road. Its top had been forcibly removed, and the liquid was covering the ground. The black liquid released an intense stench. It was...

"Gasoline?!"

"This *is* an oil drilling facility. Of course there would be refined oil around."

In total, there had to be at least sixty gallons of it.

The gasoline wasn't just pooling into a puddle. It had become as large as a small lake.

And it seemed to be surrounding Jhin and Mismis.

The five mages standing in front of them were keeping their distance from the gasoline. That meant one thing.

"They say in the past that our great Revered Founder turned the Imperial capital into a sea of flames. I think a little reprisal wouldn't be so bad."

The masked man raised both his hands.

"Think of this as the flame of our revenge!"

This was bad. The silver-haired sniper gnashed his molars.

"Boss, run! You'll get caught in the flames!"

"..."

"Boss?"

"...No!"

The blue-haired captain grabbed Jhin from behind, refusing to leave his side.

"I can't run away on my own."

"Gh."

CHAPTER 5

The poison was making Jhin's legs cramp. Lord Mask had stabbed him with a knife blade coated with astral poison that had brought about this terrible paralysis. It concentrated in his arm, then circulated to the rest of his body.

Astral poison would disappear within a few hours, but they didn't have a few seconds until they would be surrounded by fire. Mismis had gathered that.

"It's fine. Let's run."

"Liar! No, Jhin, I—"

"Love is so beautiful… But that won't save your subordinate, Miss Incompetent Little Captain."

With the moon behind him, Lord Mask snapped his fingers at the fire mage waiting behind him.

"Light it up."

Nothing happened.

"……What's going on?" Lord Mask turned around to the guards behind him with frustration. He turned to one of the four guards in particular.

"Did you not hear my order?"

"I…I am sorry…!"

It was the voice of a young girl, though it was impossible to guess the ages of any of the helmeted guards.

"…I can't produce any fire!"

"What?"

The witch wearing a hide pilot suit pulled off her glove and threw it away. There was a bright-red astral crest on the back of her hand. As though trying to appeal to Lord Mask, it glowed with power.

She was using her abilities, but no flame appeared.

"Then you—"

"I-it's the same for me...!" another sorcerer answered.

They couldn't use their astral abilities. Even though their astral crests glowed, they could barely manage to create a passing breeze.

"...Wait. *What is this wind?*" The purebred from the House of Zoa raised his face.

He had just picked up on it. The wind wasn't cold. If they were in the desert, it should have been cold enough to chill him to the bone.

But then what about this wind?

It was warm, almost like a spring breeze.

"This isn't from the desert... It can't be!"

All five pairs of the astral mages' eyes gathered to one spot... to the Imperial members there...to the Imperial soldier who was an enemy of the Nebulis Sovereignty...to the captain...and to her left shoulder.

"What is that astral crest?!"

A brilliant emerald light had appeared from Mismis's left shoulder, wrapping around her like a flowing current and spreading through the air. It had produced this wind.

The planet...had not smiled upon Lord Mask, who had used the vortex as an execution device.

It had chosen the woman whose body had been offered to the vortex.

"I see."

A cold smile seeped out from under his mask.

"I never would have guessed *you would have ended up like this* after coming back from the vortex alive. What is with this wind? I suppose it is a subspecies of wind types."

CHAPTER 5

It wasn't just any normal breeze. It must have been more than a simple gale. This didn't explain why the fire types were ineffective.

"Imperial Captain, do you even know about your astral powers?"

"—" The captain just gritted her teeth and elected not to answer.

She didn't even know what was happening herself. If anything, she hadn't understood why Lord Mask and the others had stopped their attack.

"Still in the process of *awakening*, huh." He tapped on the edge of his mask. "How curious. You have passed through the vortex's trial. Well, Imperial Captain, though I am not satisfied, it seems that the planet has chosen you."

"..."

"And your astral powers are incredibly interesting. What would you think of becoming my—?"

There was a gunshot.

Jhin had fired one bullet—which pierced the purebred's mask.

"Shut up."

Mismis was holding on to him as tightly as she could from behind.

"Don't you dare defile my boss with your dirty words," the silver-haired sniper spat out.

...*Crack*.

With a dry noise, the metal mask broke in half from the forehead and fell to the ground. Right before his bare face could be exposed, the masked man used one of his hands to cover it up.

"I see." His words were even colder than they had ever been before.

The glint of his eyes was more brilliant than the twinkle of the stars from between the gaps of his fingers.

"...It seems the time is ripe, guards. We have dillydallied too long," he said to the four guards behind him.

"Remember this," he said to the two Imperial soldiers in front of him. "This was an enjoyable little soiree. As a token of my thanks, I would like to extend an invitation to visit my lab sometime. It is an astounding room. It is completely tucked away and entirely soundproof. Your voices will never make it outside, even if you cry bloody murder."

"Is that supposed to be a threat?"

"Please let Sisbell know: She has no allies anywhere. She can never come back to her homeland."

"...Sisbell?" Jhin muttered.

The purebred didn't respond, leaving the oil drilling facility along with his subordinates.

"Did they...leave...?"

"Let's follow after Iska."

"W-wait, Jhin. We need to stop you from bleeding first!" Captain Mismis pointed at his right arm, which still dripped with blood. "Hurry and take off your jacket. We gotta stop it."

"It'll heal with a little spit."

"No, it won't! What're you saying? This is an order—"

A flame burned through the sky, surging out from the back of the grounds.

It was enormous in size.

"Huh? Wh-what was that...?"

"Is the masked man still up to no good? Wait, it came from the opposite direction... In the direction of the Object."

"Then what happened to Iska and Nene?!"

CHAPTER 5

"Boss, please stop the bleeding for me. Since we need to go ASAP, just do the bare minimum."

He picked up his sniper rifle with his left hand, which could barely move. He was angry with his legs, which were cramping from the poison.

"We're going after them, too."

3

Crackle, crackle. Flames rolled into the air, breaking like waves and spawning thousands of embers.

"...This is an oil drilling plant."

Sisbell shivered when she gazed up at the wall of fire.

"If the oil ignites from the flame, there's no saving us..."

"And it's not an issue just for us. If this place combusts, it'll be big enough to blow away the residential district on the outskirts." Iska readied himself as he swept away with his sword the embers that fell on his head.

The resort would be turned into ash overnight.

...Who in the Empire did this? Was it headquarters or the Eight Great Apostles?

...Who let someone use this atrocious weapon?

The Object...was part of a series of "Witch Hunters." This was a machine that was entirely separate and unknown to even the Empire's soldiers.

"Shifting energy. Directing line to core. Five seconds until invocation of life-form integra."

A light glowed in the open hole from its thrust-out chest.

"It's that thing from before...!"

"No way?! But any normal weapon wouldn't be able to move after releasing that amount of energy!"

As the top-rate engineer, Nene made her observation and thrust out her finger. She pointed at the Object that was currently condensing light.

"Life-form integra."

"Piercing shot!"

The armor-covered soldier kneeled.

The shell that Nene had shot from her satellite weapon had gouged a gigantic depression into its back. The flashing light had diffused.

"I did it! I barely stopped it!"

"Great timing, Nene."

It would probably need time until it could collect energy again. There was a possibility that Iska would be able to destroy the Object with his astral swords now that it had peeled off its firm outer shell.

"Release full functionality."

Iska stepped forward.

It ejected twelve satellite terminals.

It peeled off its armor—but not the incredibly thick outer crust. It released the thin inner layer of armor that clanged on the ground like silver petals.

The twelve silver pieces seemed to flutter in the wind as they started to scatter around the Object.

They looked exactly like satellites. They were like small celestial bodies revolving around a gigantic planet.

"I-it changed form again?!" Sisbell shrieked.

"Iska, stop. Those are all sensors! If you get close, it'll hit you!"

CHAPTER 5

"…What's going on, Nene?"

The girl in the ponytail once again extended her finger with the ring. She had no ammunition left. There was one thing left in the satellite weapon that could work.

"Grenade!"

A torrent of high-power explosives rained down.

These bullets, which created localized explosions, had enough destructive power to stop the Object after it had abandoned both layers of its armor.

"Life-form integra."

Twelve flashes went through the night sky. All the satellites scattered in the air glowed at the same time and burned through the falling grenades with perfect aim, causing them to evaporate into the shadows of the night.

"Did it just…shoot them down?!"

"…I knew it," Nene interjected in frustration.

They had been destroyed in the shadows of night as the high-speed grenades had come down from over their heads.

"Iska, make sure you don't get close to it! We don't know the range of those sensors yet. If you get caught up in them, you'll get burned by the lasers!"

"This is a pretty nasty weapon…"

The twelve flashes could be emitted at light speed. Even Iska wouldn't be able to dodge arrows of light.

"Nene, is there anything you can do? Do you have anything that could stop it?!"

"…If Jhin was here…," Nene said as she stared down the Object that gradually was approaching them.

"My 'star' can only drop bombs from above, but Jhin might be able to find a blind spot and snipe it."

He could locate a pin-size object that would go past all the gaps among the twelve satellites that flew through the air. The shot would require near-miraculous timing and divine talent, a transcendental technique that was arduous even to a top-rate sniper.

But Jhin could probably do it.

"Nene—"

"I know. Just hold out here, Iska. I'll go check on the captain and Jhin!"

The girl's ponytail whipped behind her. Before he could blink, she had melted into the night and, in that time, the heavy weapon approached the fence before their eyes.

Iska and Sisbell no longer had anywhere to run.

"Shifting energy. Direct source to core."

Right then, the light glowed in the middle of the Object's body.

"Fifteen seconds until invocation of life-form integra."

"It still has energy?!"

This was abnormal. It could not only release the light from each of its twelve parts but appeared to be able to release that monumental heat ray from its main body.

...If it releases it again...this'll probably be the end, regardless of whether we get hit with it or dodge!

If the laser reached the oil, it would cause a huge chain reaction. The only thing they could do was stop the Object once and for all within fifteen seconds. But because of the satellites that revolved around its body, it was like it had an impregnable defense.

"Damn..."

And what were the chances of Jhin arriving within fifteen seconds? Close to none. Zero. Even if he got there in time, he wouldn't be able to do the job in fifteen seconds. In that case, what could he do?

"Run away, Iska!" shouted the descendant of the Founder Sisbell Lou Nebulis IX.

CHAPTER 5

The sweet blond witch looked ready to do or die trying.

"...You can't die here. I've prepared myself for this."

"Sisbell?!"

"First, we need to bear through this. I will not quit here."

She could see the past. Just earlier, she had told Iska about her secret power. But how would that be useful? He really couldn't see Sisbell's power being necessary at this instant, but—

"Illumination, revive the splendor of this planet!" she sang.

Light flowed out of the witch's chest. The astral power had responded to its master's request, exhibiting its true value in that moment.

"Cosmos memory. For all the children who were once forgotten."

It passed through eternity and *summoned* the planet's past condition and sounds.

There was a gigantic sandstorm, a gale that swallowed up the Object. The wind raged, whipping around sand and gravel, and even surrounded the twelve satellites with grit.

"A sandstorm?!"

"It's an image. It is the legendary sandstorm that occurred one hundred and fifty years ago."

"...*This* is an image?!"

There was no wind, but the sand looked like it had to be real, flying around and obstructing their vision. Even the sounds of the wind had been re-created.

It didn't look like a fake sandstorm.

Even Iska hadn't realized it wasn't real until he was told.

"The true nature of Illumination is that it can 'summon natural phenomena.' It can re-create these spaces and sounds, which I've just been calling a 'video' for short."

...If she hadn't told me, I wouldn't have known... I feel like I'm being hypnotized or am hallucinating.

It would have made enemies and allies dissolve into chaos had it been used on the battlefield. The Object was no exception. Since the twelve satellites had lost their vision, their sensors had been completely obstructed.

"This is my single measure of self-defense. I haven't even shown this large-scale reproduction to the queen. Please keep it a secret." Sisbell grinned; then her mouth tensed. "We have five seconds left! You won't be targeted by the sensors! Quickly now!"

"Okay!" He dove into the sandstorm. Grains of sand filled his vision, and the roar made his eardrums almost burst.

Inside the great gale of sand, he would find the Object guarded by the satellites.

It had ejected all its armor. The mechanized soldier had become thin and delicate, as though it had the body of a human. In the middle of it, the glowing astral energy blinked as Iska aimed at it—

"I'm going for it."

He jumped off the ground.

At that moment, the Object turned around. Even in this terrible sandstorm, the twelve sensors still had been able to quickly detect him on his fast approach.

"Life-form integra."

The light twinkled.

The high-density laser pierced through the shadow approaching the Object.

But it wasn't Iska's silhouette.

It pierced through the gigantic image of a predator running next to him.

"???"

CHAPTER 5

"It's a basilisk. This desert used to be home to them, but that wasn't included as one of your inputs, Object."

The witch had revealed her trick. Sisbell hadn't just reproduced the sandstorm. She had created a projection of the beast known as the king of the desert.

The sandstorm had been meant to hide Iska's form.

The basilisk had been made to be Iska's decoy. She had produced them both.

"Knowledge is power. You should go study up on the history of this place."

There was a flash.

Iska had destroyed the Object's center with perfect aim, using his astral sword.

"—" The mechanized soldier fell down faceup. When its back hit the hard ground, the light in the gigantic hole in its chest was extinguished.

Then it stopped moving.

"W-we beat it…"

"Somehow. But it was a lot stronger than I thought it'd be."

But they couldn't *just* beat it. Now they had to use some sort of trick to make it look as though the Sovereign mages had destroyed the Object. There were the traces of Iska's blade attacks in the soldier's chest. There was a gigantic hole from the shells that Nene had shot at its back. They needed to hide those marks.

"And we need to check what's inside it."

He looked down at the soldier that did not so much as twitch.

"You saw it, too, right? That light from inside it."

"…It looked like astral energy."

"That's what I thought. It wasn't from electricity."

Should they examine the combustion engine? It wouldn't be

long before Nene would be back with Jhin and Captain Mismis. With her, they would be able to—

"*Movement impossible. Ejecting core of* ▪▪▪▪▪."

They heard an automated sound. Iska felt a chill down his spine when he could detect something coming from inside the incapacitated soldier.

What was this uncanny feeling?!

"Wh-what is that light…? It's a flame!" Sisbell rasped.

From the gaps between the machine and its wires, they could see bright-blue flames lapping up like steam. The astral energy that had once disappeared was burning again.

…And it was surging even stronger than before.

…I don't know what's happening… I can't take my time trying to figure out what this thing is!

They were in danger. His body alerted him, breaking into a cold sweat.

"Get away!"

"Y-yes!"

They started to run at the same time.

But, after taking just a few steps, the girl fell onto her knees. With her lifestyle in the palace, her legs had reached their limits after she had scampered down the rough paths.

"W-wait, Iska!"

"…Sisbell?!" He turned around when the girl screamed.

All of it was too late by then. The light seeping out from the soldier had reached its critical limit.

"Help me—"

Something flared.

The explosion expanded as though it were engulfing the entire area.

* * *

CHAPTER 5

"What do you think you're doing to my sister?"

"*Freeze.*"

That had given way to a wall of ice. It was one of the most mesmerizing barriers in the world. It towered over Iska and Sisbell like a castle wall. It held back the surging flames and made the heat wave disappear before they could blink.

"...Alice?!"

"I found you, Sisbell."

It was Aliceliese Lou Nebulis IX.

With her older sister exposed to the desert wind, Sisbell opened her eyes wide.

"Wh-why are you here?"

"Because I had something I needed to discuss with you. But we can save that for later... Iska, what's going on here?"

Out of breath, Alice turned around. She faced the Imperial swordsman who held his sword in his hand.

The Ice Calamity Witch Alice knew Iska had fought to capture a purebred himself as the Successor of the Black Steel.

In other words, was Iska the Imperial soldier targeting her sister?

"It *wasn't* you."

Alice stared down Iska and scowled.

Sisbell's enemy wasn't Iska. Sisbell herself was nestled up against his back as though she was hiding.

"Catch me up. I want to know what just happened."

"Can't you tell?"

Beyond the extinguished flame and smoke was a dull object crawling on the ground. It was indigo with a glowing humanoid silhouette. That was the Object's core.

The core's entire body was radiating light similar to astral energy.

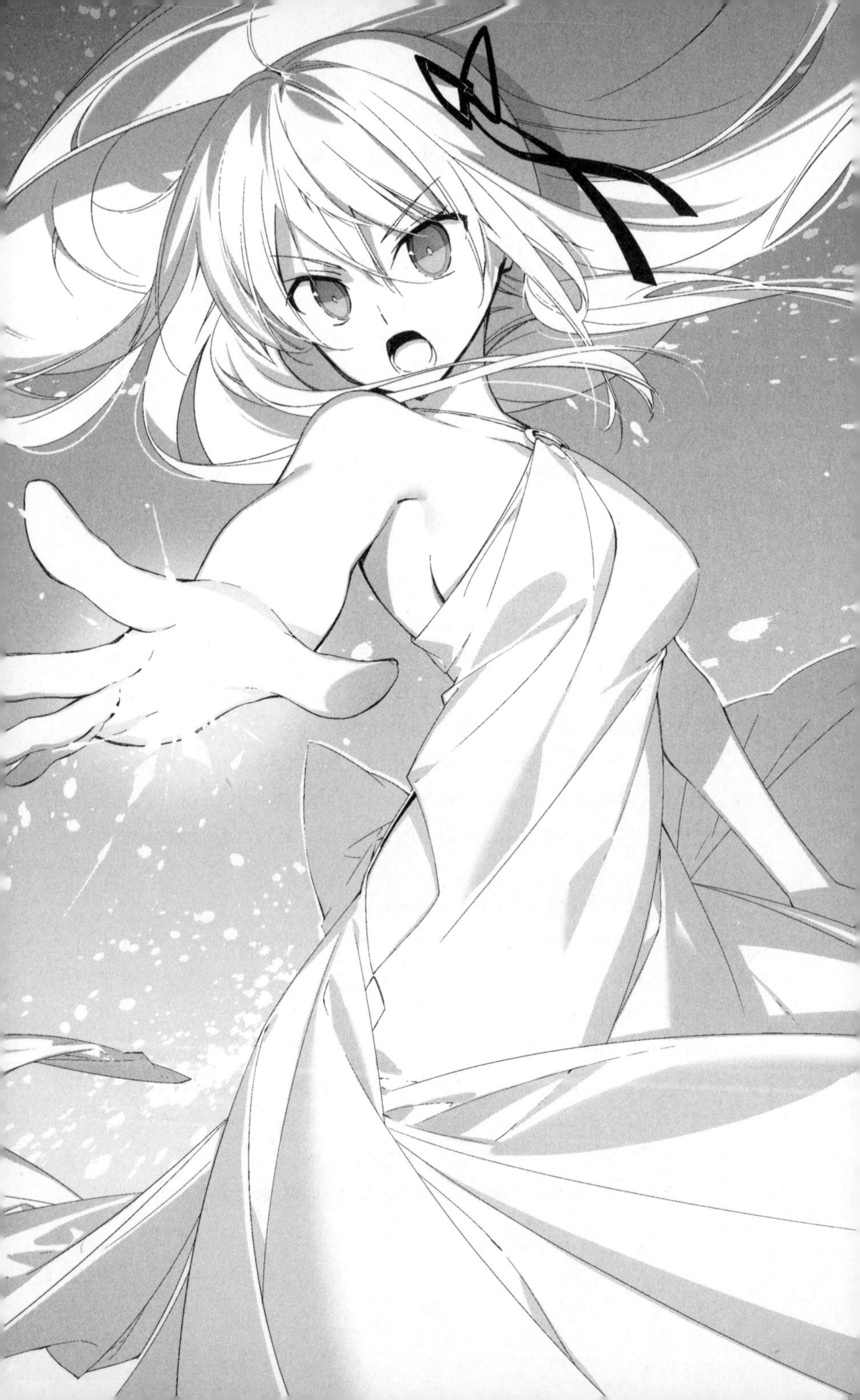

CHAPTER 5

"Does that thing look like our ally?" Iska asked.

"...I'm glad it's so obvious. Anyway, I think our top priority is battling that ghost."

Alice nodded calmly and turned to the glowing form.

A ghost.

That certainly was a fitting comparison for the humanoid silhouette, which glowed dimly. But what was the nature of its glow, which reminded them of astral energy?

"We just need to beat it quickly, don't we? In that case, I'll—"

"Shifting energy."

The glowing humanoid thrust out the palm of its hand at Alice.

"Preparing to invoke life-form integra."

"Oh no! Aliceliese, run!" shouted Sisbell.

"Huh?" Alice blinked. "What are you talking about, Sisbell? I can easily clean up this guy—"

"Alice!" Iska yelled at the princess of the enemy nation. She wouldn't make it in time. Even if Alice tried running now, her speed wouldn't allow her to escape from the laser's aim.

"Your flower! Make it bloom!"

"Wh-what are you talking about, Iska? That's one of my secrets. I can't so easily..."

"Hurry!"

Her "ice flower" was a secret. She had reservations about exhibiting it outside the battlefield. However, her trust in her rival trumped her hesitation.

—This is Iska. There definitely has to be a reason for this request.

"Life-form integra."

"Bloom!"

With faint reverberations of a clear *shling*, she had created the most spellbinding shield in the world. This was the true nature of the ice flower that dwelled in Aliceliese Lou Nebulis IX. It manifested itself as a beautiful flower.

The shield stopped the laser that had even managed to melt a gigantic crane and sent the light flying to the side.

"...Amazing! Of course my sister would be."

"—"

"Aliceliese?" Sisbell gulped back her saliva and watched.

The lips of Alice herself were pale as ice. Had she been even slightly late when creating the flower, her entire body would have been blasted away by the light. There wouldn't have been a method of protecting herself other than invoking the ice flower like Iska had told her. She had narrowly survived.

"...I was off my guard." Her eyes suddenly narrowed. "I was off my game because this wasn't the battlefield."

Alice's expression shifted to one of the Ice Calamity Witch, the purebred feared by the Empire.

"Sisbell, stay back. This opponent is dangerous, so I'm going to end things in one hit."

She pointed at the Object.

She wouldn't hold back, meeting it with her entire source of energy. The Object's behavior in response to Alice's will to fight was out of their expectations.

"Remaining energy reaching lower limit."

"...?"

"Counting down from ten."

They heard an automated noise. As the Object floated over the asphalt road, Iska bit his lip, looking up at it over his head.

...Nene was right... There's no way a single weapon could keep releasing this much energy.

The Object didn't have any power left. There was only one

decision that the Eight Great Apostles would have made for a weapon that had completed its purpose.

"It's going to self-destruct!"

"What?!"

"...What did you say?!"

Their faces froze. This was an oil drilling facility. They had no idea of the scale of the explosion, but they did know it would definitely have enough power to blow away the warehouses.

The blaze would go out in all directions. It wasn't an explosion that even Alice could hold back instantaneously.

"Eight... Seven—"

Because of that, she needed to completely destroy it before the countdown ended. Iska and Alice reached the same conclusion without needing to say a single word.

"Ice Calamity—Fan Dance of a Thousand Swords!"

Thousands of blue shots materialized, creating extremely low-temperature ice bullets in the night sky. Lights twinkling like powder snow came down, covering the Object's entire body.

They weren't any ordinary bullets. Alice's technique was nearly at absolute zero. The chill was close to the point that molecular motion would cease. It had frozen and stopped the air around the glowing body, but—

"Five... Four..."

The countdown continued.

"I hate to admit this, but we have no time... Iska! Over there!"

"I know." Iska was already running to the place where the witch had turned. "You mean *this fence*, right?"

The fence had been frosted over with Alice's blue shots. He jumped on top of it and used it as a way of leaping even higher into the air.

As a fence, it wouldn't have been firm enough for him to launch himself off, but with Alice's ice, the fence was resilient enough to support him.

That wasn't a coincidence. It was all a part of the Ice Calamity Witch's calculation and the Successor of the Black Steel had implicitly read her motives.

"*Three... Two—*"

"This is it."

The swordsman crossed through the air.

His astral blade was absorbed into the night and cut through the frozen Object.

It ruptured with particles of light.

There was no explosion.

As Iska landed, the night sky slowly returned back to its inky black color. They looked up at that scene from the ground.

"...I just don't understand," Alice said, obviously peeved. "All I want is to settle things with you instead of fighting together. Why do we always end up in situations that could be misunderstood?"

They were in the independent state of Alsamira. Though it wasn't as if the state had banned combat like the neutral cities, the two countries couldn't battle each other directly.

If Iska and Alice were to use their full force to fight, they would cause serious damage to the oil drilling plant. As a Sovereign princess, Alice wasn't after that.

"Well, it's fine... Besides, I don't see any other Imperial soldiers around here anyway." She sighed. "Iska, I'd like you to tell me what's going on. What are you doing with this girl in this place late at night?"

CHAPTER 5

"Aliceliese." Sisbell had pulled on her sister's skirt from behind.

"You may wait, Sisbell. I'm talking with Iska right now—"

"Do you know who this Imperial soldier is?"

"Oh..."

Alice came back to her senses.

She barely stopped herself from saying, *Uh-oh*. But her face was an open book. She had ended up acting as though she was close to Iska because she had been so caught up in the state of affairs.

"I knew it." Sisbell's eyes narrowed with distrust.

"Why would you know this Imperial soldier when you are a Sovereign princess? You know him well enough to call him by his name."

"..."

"This has bothered me for some time. What kind of relationship do you have with him?"

"..." Alice gulped and held her breath. "I don't know him at all. *Who are you?* Oh, I'm sure you must be Sisbell's guard." She turned to Iska.

"Huh?! B-but...?!"

"Alice?!"

—*Just get with the program! You'd be under suspicion for knowing a Sovereign princess!* Alice begged him desperately with her eyes as she turned her back on her sister.

This was a matter of life and death. If headquarters suspected Iska had contact with Alice, they would imprison him again. If the royal family knew Alice had been in contact with Iska, that would put her in a precarious position.

They needed to keep things private.

"Isn't that right?"

"...Oh yeah—totally! I had no idea who you were, either. Ha-ha...ha..."

"Could you please give up this act?" Sisbell's voice was stern. "Didn't you just call him 'Iska'?"

"I heard you call him by his name. Plus, look at the situation we're in. Of course I would talk to this swordsman thinking he was your guard."

"...So you're going to feign ignorance."

"I have no idea what you're talking about."

Sisbell's expression was cold, which the older sister pretended not to notice. Iska was in front of them, watching.

"I see. So you do not know him, right?" Sisbell asked.

"That's right. I have not a single clue about his identity."

"Works for me."

"...Huh?"

"You hear that, Iska?" Princess Sisbell broke into a victorious smile. Before Alice could figure out what it meant, she had made her way right in front of Iska. "I have confirmed it through that battle, Iska. I have made no mistake in judgment."

She took Iska's hand. The Sovereign princess's eyes glistened.

"I will not give up until I make you my subordinate! I will absolutely make sure you join me—I pledge on my name of Sisbell Lou Nebulis IX as the next queen."

"Stop right there!" Alice shouted.

She stood in front of Iska to block Sisbell and pulled her sister away from him by force.

"Wh-wh-wh-wh-what do you think you're saying, Sisbell?!"

"This has nothing to do with you, dear sister." Sisbell seemed triumphant. "Iska will join my side."

"This is no joking matter. Iska is mine! He's my rival! Right?"

"...Uh, well, you're the one who asked me to feign ignorance, Alice."

CHAPTER 5

Sandwiched between Alice and Sisbell, he had no idea how to respond.

"Iska?" called out Nene from the asphalt. Pairs of footsteps followed. That must have been Jhin and Captain Mismis.

...This is bad!

...If they see this, everyone is going to be suspicious of me this time!

Iska turned his back on Alice and Sisbell, who were glaring at each other.

"Sorry, guys. My friends are calling, so I'm heading off."

"Huh?! Wait, Iska!"

"Iska, I'm not going to give up! Never!"

He ran away from that place as fast as he could, putting distance between the two sisters.

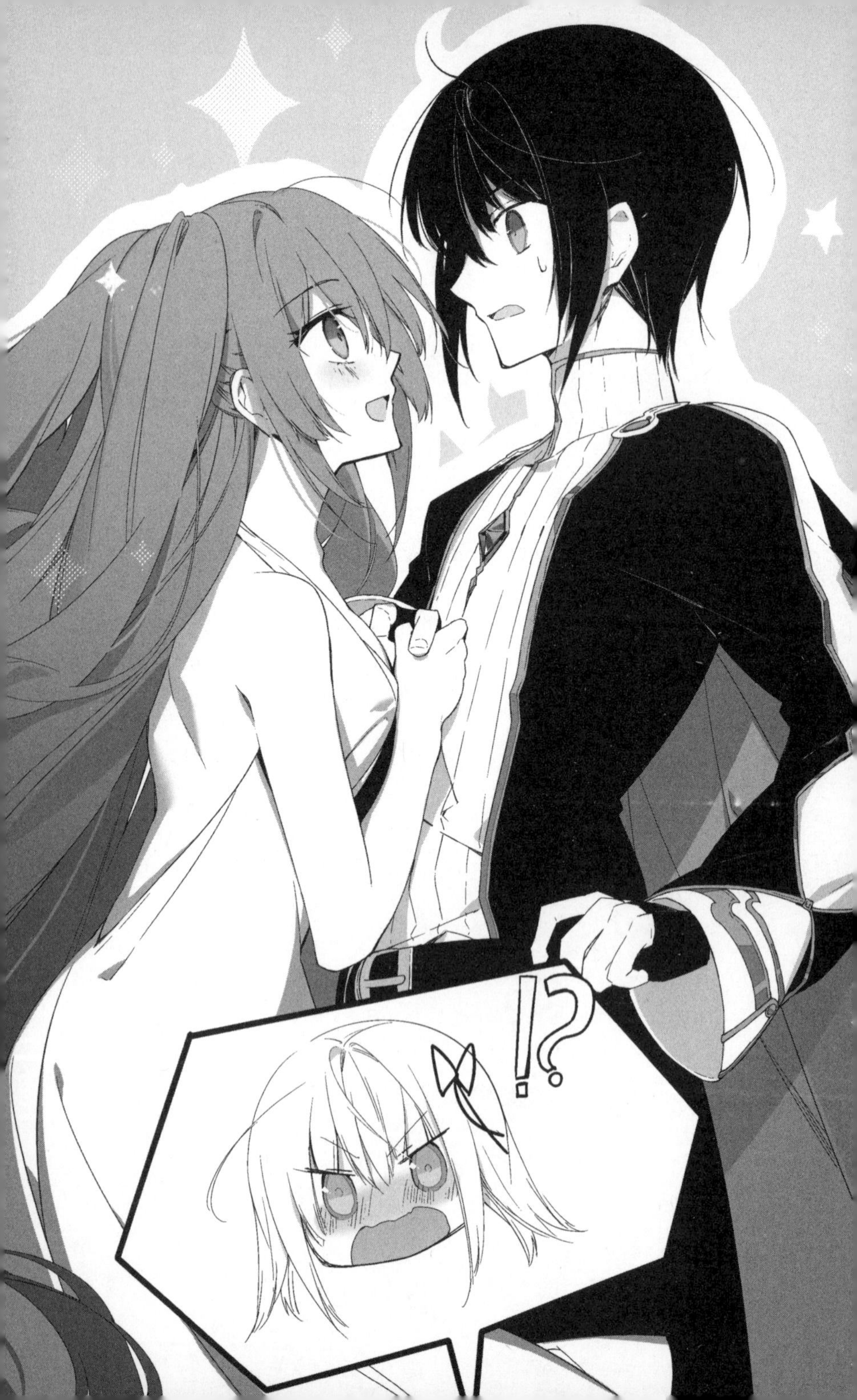

INTERMISSION

In Exchange for Power

The Nebulis Sovereignty. The eighth state of Wreathbarden.

The state ran adjacent to the Sovereign border, said to be the birthplace of world literature inspired from interactions with the neutral cities.

Its beautifully maintained streets were teeming with people leisurely going along their way.

There was not a single cloud in the sky. Many groups of women were enjoying a momentary afternoon meal on the outside seating areas of cafés facing the square.

But this café was currently filled with commotion. A man had appeared in the full seating area. His beautiful form was enough to instantly eliminate all forms of drowsiness.

"—"

The man silently sat down at an empty seat.

His pale face was chiseled. His gaze was sharp. His pursed lips displayed a solemnity that indicated he would never waver in the face of anything.

Conspicuous and tall, the man had a buff and bare chest that was covered by a single coat.

It was like an act in a play.

Though he had only sat down, the young women and older ladies were prisoners to his allure and imposing conduct.

"S-sir...your order...?"

"—"

When the blushing waitress attended to him, the man silently pointed at the menu.

"R-right at once!"

He didn't even look at the waitress as she rushed into the café. The man with white hair brought out a report about a dozen pages long. He carefully started reading the report written in unintelligible jargon.

"...This is getting on my last nerve," the man said in a voice with suppressed vigor.

Salinger.

Thirty years prior, the "transcendental" sorcerer had instigated an unprecedented incident by single-handedly charging the royal palace to turn his blade on the queen. Though he should have easily been a fifty-year-old man, his body, face, and vengeance were all at their prime rather than in decay. He still had more room for growth.

"A-apologies for the delay!"

"..." He practically flicked the payment and tip at the waitress when she brought out the coffee and soufflé pancakes.

"Yunmelngen. That monster," Salinger muttered in irritation. "Just when the throne appeared in front of me, it turned out to be a delusion. I never would have expected that scoundrel to force these records on me."

He had a top secret document issued about a particular

INTERMISSION

"research device" in the Empire. Naturally, bringing the documents out of the facility was prohibited. With the exception of one person: the symbol of the Empire, Yunmelngen, the one with the highest political authority.

Experiment Results:
Administered weakened ■■■■ *on a witch with congenital* ■■*. Favorable results seen when administered on purebred "Specimen E."*

"'Specimen E,' huh? There are only two people I can think of."

He thought about the names and faces of all the Founder's descendants who lurked in the royal palace.

"Why should I care?"

Salinger balled up the report in his hands, burning it in his palm and turning it into ash so that it blew away in the wind. He watched that absentmindedly without much emotion.

"...Hmm?" The handsome white-haired man suddenly noticed the young girl immediately next to him.

She stared. But she wasn't gaping at Salinger. Her gaze was focused on the soufflé pancakes on the table. She must have smelled them after they had come straight from the pan.

"What do you want, girl?"

"Hey, mister, are you going to eat those? If you're not, can I have them?"

How frank.

It must have been because of her age. Give her a few more years, and she would learn how to coax people with a courteous smile and friendly tone.

"I have two things to tell you," the sorcerer replied, disgusted. "One, I do not enjoy being called by a pandering title. Two, I paid for this. Do not beg. Anything you obtain comes at a price."

"..." The girl turned her face down.

"You must have money."

She had a money pouch tied around her neck with a string. She couldn't be broke.

"I haven't got any money in it."

"Hmm?"

"It's a shiny rock. I got it at the riverbed." The young girl flipped open her change purse.

Don't pour it over my table— Before Salinger could stop her, she had already scattered tiny rocks all around his coffee cup. They were faintly tinted and striped.

"Onyx stones, huh. They are nothing significant." Salinger picked up one incredibly small and round rock without heed.

"Oh! No. That's my—"

"This will do."

"...What?"

"This will due in exchange. But make sure you find a nicer rock next time."

He turned his back on the girl, whose face had gone blank, and started walking. He left the entire plate of soufflé pancakes on the table.

"But your exchange won't be so cheap, my queen," he spat. "You obtained the throne of queen with luck. Unfortunately for you, you have no idea of the true price of obtaining the throne."

He headed straight onto a small, dark road that continued along to alleys. The sun did not shine here.

"Have fun with what remains of your rule. The bloodline of the Founder... A true monster will soon be at your throat."

The sorcerer sauntered to the central state, to the castle where the royal family of Nebulis gathered.

EPILOGUE

Whose Is This?

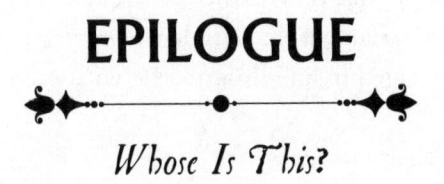

1

"Fifteen minutes. Any more than that, and the others will get suspicious."

"I know."

They were in the independent state of Alsamira. Tucked away in a corner of the resting area set up in a gigantic shopping mall, Iska and Alice were sitting at a bench together.

They might have been mistaken for a couple by the people around them, but the two in question wore concerned expressions on their faces.

"...I just want to confirm what we talked about earlier."

Alice was close enough that he could have touched her shoulder. The silky strands of her blond hair were on his shoulder, and he felt uneasy about the unfamiliar sensation.

...Ugh, focus... My life is on the line here.

He tried his best not to look at Alice's face from the side.

"You found an article talking about me hidden in Sisbell's room?"

"Yes. She must be suspicious about our relations. I suspect she thinks I'm a princess with ties to the Empire."

But it wasn't that they had connections. Had this been the battlefield rather than within an independent state, Iska and Alice would have engaged in an all-out battle with each other without a word.

That was their fate.

The two of them were enemies. They were rivals. They had no intention of colluding with each other.

"...But I wonder why I always meet you in places like this."

"...That's what I should be saying."

They weren't betraying their countries. They were both fighting for the sake of them. It would be an incredible nuisance if anyone misunderstood and thought otherwise.

"That's why I need to reconfirm this. I want you to pretend you don't know me in front of anyone from the Sovereignty. Even in front of Sisbell."

"I think that'd make her super suspicious, though."

"Do it regardless. The worst thing that could happen would be if she found out about the neutral city of Ain. And that goes for both you and me."

"...I got it. But is there one thing I can ask you about?"

"You may."

"Isn't she your little sister?"

Couldn't Alice honestly tell Sisbell about the circumstances surrounding Iska? He just couldn't wrap his head around that.

"Yes, but..."

"But?"

"Only one of us can become queen."

"Uh."

EPILOGUE

"I am conflicted about that, too. Last night, I was absorbed in looking for her and came running over. But for one moment...I almost felt regretful. Why did I save her? If I hadn't, there would have been one less successor to the throne."

Her gaze was tinged with grief before something made it flip to rage.

"It is an embarrassment. I am pitiful for even letting that cross my mind for a moment. The throne of the queen shouldn't be obtained through underhanded measures. In order to be fully accepted and followed by the people and the royal family— ... Oh......"

The princess came to her senses and stopped talking. She turned her eyes away from Iska as though she was shy.

"I-I'm sorry. I shouldn't be telling this to an Imperial soldier..."

Then she stood up, looking down at Iska, who was still sitting on the bench.

"This is a deal... I don't think the occasion will occur often, but I would like you to stop talking about me."

"Even if I get caught by the astral corps and tortured?"

The blond girl bent down so she could look directly into his eyes.

"In exchange, I will keep one of your important secrets hidden."

"What's that?"

What important secret? Iska couldn't think of anything that was more important than these meetings with Alice. Was there something else that Alice would intentionally insinuate?

"*Your captain has turned into a witch. Isn't that right?*"

"...Uh!" He instinctively stood up.

"It must have happened when she fell into the vortex. I even know her crest is on her left shoulder."

"...You knew about all that?"

When and where had she found out this information? But Alice was a princess of the Paradise of Witches. She had to be more sensitive to astral power than someone from the Empire.

...She went out of her way to use the word witch*... She wants to imply what would happen if that spread across the Empire.*

If it was disclosed that a commander in the Imperial Army had turned into a witch, Unit 907 would come crashing down on itself.

"So you get it? We both have each other's secrets."

"...Yeah." His shoulders slumped. "Nothing will leave this conversation."

"That's right. Let's keep this our little secret... Ha-ha. My heart is racing. It's like we're equals in this relationship."

"Why're you happy about this?"

"I-I'm not! You're so rude! I'm trying to have a serious conversation." Alice suddenly swept away her bangs and cleared her throat. "I have something I must discuss with Sisbell. Well, then—"

"Yeah, *see you around.*"

The witch princess turned to leave, sweeping her hair through the air. He watched her graceful silhouette from behind.

"I should get going, too. I'm making the captain wait."

Iska was starting to leave.

"...But I'm conflicted. Should I stay in this country or go somewhere else?"

2

Alice took a step out of the shopping mall where she had left Iska.

"Phew! It's so hot outside. Maybe I should have brought a parasol..."

EPILOGUE

The blinding sunlight made Alice narrow her eyes. This was Alsamira, the desert of tourists. Unlike the night, the temperature would become a scorching heat by midday.

"My dear sister Aliceliese." Sisbell had come to her wearing a cute sun hat.

"Oh, where did that come from?"

"I just bought it. I thought it would act as a bit of a disguise." She pulled the large brim of the hat low over her eyes.

"Because Lord Mask is looking for you?"

"—" Sisbell was silent.

Nothing about this was different from their usual interactions. Alice had hoped her sister would open up now that they were finally outside the palace, but Sisbell kept her mouth shut just like always.

...But now one suspicion has been cleared... When Sisbell confided in me last night.

It was that during the incident where Iska helped a witch escape jail, he had saved Sisbell. She'd had the magazine tucked away because she had been looking into the Imperial soldier from that event.

She hadn't been suspicious of the relationship between Alice and Iska.

But *Alice had not heard about Sisbell being captured by the Empire*—from within the royal palace.

Someone had control over the flow of information.

If Sisbell had disappeared, no one in the palace would have noticed, since she was usually cooped up in her room.

...I wonder if our mother knows? ...If she did know, she never would have allowed Sisbell to come to this country alone.

How had Sisbell even been captured in the first place?

There was no way that her sister could have been captured in an Imperial prison unless Sisbell had left the Sovereignty and gone into Imperial territory herself.

And then there were the events that had just occurred. How had the Imperial Army found out that a purebred would be in this country?

"Sisbell, there's something I'd like to ask you."

"Aliceliese," Sisbell answered indifferently. "I believe I already told you at the hotel last night. One year ago, I made a mistake, which caused me to get caught by the Empire. He saved me while I was imprisoned."

"Yes, but—"

"That's all I can tell you about."

"What?! Sisbell! Wait! Wait for me!"

"I'm busy. I have a mission that I received from our mother. Please go back home to our country ahead of me. Isn't that Salinger still on the run? I think you should really return to the castle quickly."

"...Uh?!"

Sisbell was still unfriendly to her sister.

But last night, she had been so alive when she had closed in on Iska and taken his hand to ask him to work with her.

It was as though...she cared for the Imperial soldier more than her own sister.

"Sisbell, listen to me! When you get back to the royal palace, you'll have a lot of questions to answer!"

"Whatever. Let's head out, Shuvalts."

Leading along the older gentleman who acted as her keeper, Sisbell walked briskly into the sea of people.

"...What will I tell my mother?" Alice sighed to herself.

It didn't take them long to get out of the shopping zone.

EPILOGUE

"My lady! I am relieved. What about your reply to Lady Alice...?"

"It's fine." Sisbell flatly shook her head at the keeper who walked next to her.

"I believe she said she came to this country worried about you. I think she is here to see you."

"Yes."

Alice had saved her from the self-destructing Object. That was true.

But she still had her doubts.

"Lord Mask?!"

"Just on a holiday."

The only ones who knew she had gone on this trip were the House of Lou.

...Lord Mask, your act won't work on me... Either Alice or Elletear fed you that information!

The Object must have also been weaponized by the same person.

One of her sisters was the informant.

One of them had to be a traitor to their country, a friend of "that monster." One of them was treacherous and had targeted their mother's life so she could be in the top position in the Sovereignty.

"Shuvalts, I still have my suspicions about my sister Alice."

What was the true reason for Alice visiting this country? Could she have come because she was secretly connected to Lord Mask, working with him on a plan to trap Sisbell?

...But they made a mistake with Iska... Did my sister jump ship and pretend to be my ally?

Sisbell had to be hypervigilant. She couldn't open her heart up to Alice yet.

"Shuvalts, I have realized something on my trip. I am in need of a guard. I need someone who can battle for me."

"I have no objections."

"And I have already decided on the person. It should definitely be Iska—"

She silently gripped her hand into a fist. When she had held his hand in the night, it had been warm.

"I definitely will not give up. I need you. Fortunately, I can be useful to you as well."

She put her hand to her chest and over her astral crest.

Her dress was currently open at the front, but no one had noticed the mark, which she had skillfully covered with a bandage, made with a special film that not only covered the light from an astral crest but could also blockade its astral energy.

It was a new material that the Empire hadn't developed yet. It was useless to Iska himself, but…

"*Your commander* needs this, doesn't she?"

Another secret relationship would bind the Imperial swordsman Iska to the witches, launching him on a different path toward his destiny.

CONTINUED

Elletear

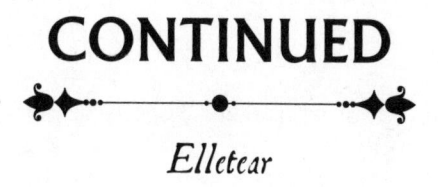

The royal palace of Nebulis. Inside the queen's room.

The serene light filtered through lace into the reception hall. The sacred space was decorated with indoor plants, sunlight, and a wine-colored carpet.

Clack... The demure sound of footsteps echoed as a beautiful princess walked forward.

"Good morning, Your Highness."

"Good morning, Elletear." Queen Mirabella stood on top of a staircase about twenty steps long and turned to her beloved daughter—the eldest of the sisters, Elletear.

"I'm sorry for calling you early in the morning after you've just returned from an extended excursion."

"I returned several days ago. I have so much energy," the eldest daughter answered with a smile before looking around the space as though she had just noticed. "Your Highness. I do not see the usual faces?"

"I have asked the guards and retainers to step out. I wanted to be alone with you."

"Oh, and why would that be?"

The queen answered her oldest daughter, who exalted her with a smile. "There are two questions I have for you."

"I will answer any."

"Were you the one who leaked Sisbell's destination?"

With her smile still plastered on her face, Elletear had frozen as though she could no longer move.

Queen Mirabella remained silent. She looked down at her daughter at the bottom of the stairs with unusually cold eyes.

"And I have one other question."

The oldest daughter said not a single word, but the queen paid her no mind.

"Are you *the real Elletear*?"

"—"

The reception hall went still. For a few seconds, her question rang faintly, until it could no longer be heard.

And then the eldest princess burst into laughter.

Afterword

A girl who can see the entire history of the planet...

    The youngest princess, Sisbell, has joined the war.

    If you remembered her from the first volume or if you were waiting in anticipation for her reappearance, I hope you are pleased by this. She had been trying to find an opportunity to shine since the beginning of Volume 1. It would make me happy if you cheered her on.

    Thank you so very much for picking up this book, *Our Last Crusade or the Rise of a New World*, Volume 4! I wanted the theme to be centered around secret relationships.

    Bound to the fate of the planet, the destinies between Iska and Alice and between Iska and Sisbell are starting to come together. Neither of these relationships can get out to the public. How will they change? Here's what might be in store in the next volume.

AFTERWORD

Sisbell will become close (to Iska).
Alice will be enraged (about Iska).
Sibling War I will break out.

Those are the key pieces of the plot, but stick around until Volume 5 to see how it plays out.

I have a happy announcement to make.

I started this series in spring of last year and received support from many people. This year, we're making even greater strides.

There will be adaptations of this story in an audio drama and a manga. And it will be serialized in *Dragon Magazine*!

First, the audio drama!

Using an original short story written by me, professional voice actors will breathe life into Iska and Alice by way of vocal performance.

Iska will be played by Yusuke Kobayashi and Alice will be played by Sora Amemiya.

Both of them are skilled actors. I was allowed to observe their recording sessions…and they are perfect for their roles. The end product is full of life and fun.

It is free for the public. Please listen to it when you have the chance.

It is being displayed on Fantasia Bunko's official site on the series page.

Now, about the manga!

It will be serialized in *Young Animal* magazine starting May 11th.

The illustrator will be Okama.

They have been very meticulous, drawing characters in their own style and trying to be informed of the details about Imperial

AFTERWORD

buildings and the wastelands outside the borders. We added some flair to certain conversations that benefitted from a visual element. Even as the author, I am hyped about this manga.

It will be serialized starting in May. I hope you'll look forward to the serialization and published volumes.

And lastly, a serialization in *Dragon Magazine*!

This will also begin in the May edition. I will be writing a short story for the series. I would like to write scenes that show the unexpected sides of the characters, but that might not work well in the longer series.

I'll put my best into writing those short stories!

And so, that concludes three projects across media.

I want to thank everyone who has rooted for me.

I want to extend my gratitude for my illustrator Ao Nekonabe and my managing editor K. Thank you, as always, for your help.

Sisbell is adorable on the cover, and I would like you to keep drawing more of her in the stories.

Volume 5 will come out sometime in summer.

I hope you are looking forward to finding out what happens in this little sibling rivalry...

And since summer is some time away, I would like to introduce my other series as something to read in the meantime.

Published by MF Bunko J, *Why Doesn't Anyone Remember My World?*

An epic about a boy who is forgotten by the rest of the world, fighting against angels, demons, mythical beasts, and other powerful species as he tries to restore "true" history in a world where it's been rewritten.

It's a relatively new series. The third volume just came out, and

AFTERWORD

the series has been doing well. It is being turned into a manga and a game. The manga serialization has already started in Kadokawa's monthly magazine, *Comic Alive*.

It's very exciting, so I hope you'll check out the book at your bookstores!

I don't have much space left.

This is a story about the swordsman Iska and the witch princess Alice.

What planetary fate surrounds the two who violently clash but are mysteriously drawn to each other?

I plan on upping the ante, now that a new witch, Sisbell, is finally joining the battle and bringing trouble to the palace of Nebulis.

Until next time.

Encore Volume 4 coming out June 25 (MF Bunko J).

Our Last Crusade or the Rise of a New World, Volume 5 will be coming out sometime in summer.

I hope that we meet again in both.

With hints of the end of spring,
Kei Sazane

https://twitter.com/sazanek

I occasionally make posts about publication announcements on Twitter.

Announcement: VOLUME 5

"Iska and I are of one body and soul."

"If you weren't my sister, I would challenge you to a duel…"

Sisbell's proposed negotiation means Iska needs to enter the Sovereignty again as her guard. Aliceliese's heart practically jumps out of her chest when she spots them together. But to accomplish their respective goals, it is imperative they pretend not to know each other.

In Volume 5, someone from the bloodline of the founder slumbering in the conclave rises to bare their fangs… at the sisters intent on sabotaging each other.

❖ The content of this book is subject to change without advance notice.

Our Last CRUSADE OR THE RISE OF A New World

VOLUME 5

Coming soon

HAVE YOU BEEN TURNED ON TO LIGHT NOVELS YET?

IN STORES NOW!

SWORD ART ONLINE, VOL. 1-20
SWORD ART ONLINE PROGRESSIVE 1-6

The chart-topping light novel series that spawned the explosively popular anime and manga adaptations!

MANGA ADAPTATION AVAILABLE NOW!

SWORD ART ONLINE © Reki Kawahara ILLUSTRATION: abec
KADOKAWA CORPORATION ASCII MEDIA WORKS

ACCEL WORLD, VOL. 1-22

Prepare to accelerate with an action-packed cyber-thriller from the bestselling author of *Sword Art Online*.

MANGA ADAPTATION AVAILABLE NOW!

ACCEL WORLD © Reki Kawahara ILLUSTRATION: HIMA
KADOKAWA CORPORATION ASCII MEDIA WORKS

SPICE AND WOLF, VOL. 1-21

A disgruntled goddess joins a traveling merchant in this light novel series that inspired the *New York Times* bestselling manga.

MANGA ADAPTATION AVAILABLE NOW!

SPICE AND WOLF © Isuna Hasekura ILLUSTRATION: Jyuu Ayakura
KADOKAWA CORPORATION ASCII MEDIA WORKS

IS IT WRONG TO TRY TO PICK UP GIRLS IN A DUNGEON?, VOL. 1-14

A would-be hero turns damsel in distress in this hilarious send-up of sword-and-sorcery tropes.

MANGA ADAPTATION AVAILABLE NOW!

Is It Wrong to Try to Pick Up Girls in a Dungeon? © Fujino Omori / SB Creative Corp.

ANOTHER

The spine-chilling horror novel that took Japan by storm is now available in print for the first time in English—in a gorgeous hardcover edition.

MANGA ADAPTATION AVAILABLE NOW!

Another © Yukito Ayatsuji 2009/ KADOKAWA CORPORATION, Tokyo

A CERTAIN MAGICAL INDEX, VOL. 1-22

Science and magic collide as Japan's most popular light novel franchise makes its English-language debut.

MANGA ADAPTATION AVAILABLE NOW!

A CERTAIN MAGICAL INDEX © Kazuma Kamachi
ILLUSTRATION: Kiyotaka Haimura
KADOKAWA CORPORATION ASCII MEDIA WORKS

VISIT YENPRESS.COM TO CHECK OUT ALL THE TITLES IN OUR NEW LIGHT NOVEL INITIATIVE AND...

GET YOUR YEN ON!

YEN ON | Yen Press

www.YenPress.com

THE Eminence IN Shadow

ONE BIG FAT LIE
AND A FEW TWISTED TRUTHS

Even in his past life, Cid's dream wasn't to become a protagonist or a final boss. He'd rather lie low as a minor character until it's prime time to reveal he's a mastermind...or at least, do the next best thing—pretend to be one! And now that he's been reborn into another world, he's ready to set the perfect conditions to live out his dreams to the fullest. Cid jokingly recruits members to his organization and makes up a whole backstory about an evil cult that they need to take down. Well, as luck would have it, these imaginary adversaries turn out to be the real deal—and everyone knows the truth but him!

YEN ON
For more information visit www.yenpress.com

IN STORES NOW!

KAGE NO JITSURYOKUSHA NI NARITAKUTE !
©Daisuke Aizawa 2018 Illustration: Touzai / KADOKAWA CORPORATION